D1193885

Visiting Miss Pierce

Visiting
Miss Pierce

■

Pat Derby

FARRAR · STRAUS · GIROUX

New York

Copyright © 1986 Pat Derby
All rights reserved
First edition, 1986
Published simultaneously in Canada
by Collins Publishers, Toronto
Printed in the United States of America
Designed by Claudia Carlson
Library of Congress catalog card number: 86–7559

To my husband,
PAUL,
and my mother,
ANGELA LYNCH,
with love

Visiting Miss Pierce

· 1 ·

I got an A in my Bay Area social concerns class. I know I shouldn't complain about getting an A, since I usually get C's, but I really felt Miss Pierce deserved it, not me. When I started to write my final paper, I tried to sort it all out and quickly realized I couldn't tell Ms. Jackson everything that had happened. It was just too weird. That's why I'm writing it all down now, so maybe then I'll be able to forget about Willie and Alice and the baby.

First, you better know who I am. My name is Barry Wilson. I'm fourteen years old, and I'm five foot three and two-fifths inches tall. My dad's an architect and my mom's a housewife and I'm adopted. I don't remember that part, because I was a baby when it happened. I do remember when Mom and Dad first told me. They said they had picked me out especially, and how wonderful it was they didn't have to take whatever comes along the way natural parents do, and other dopey things like that. I guess I didn't understand what they were talking about, because after that I thought they had bought me at a store. I was seven or eight before I really understood what being adopted was all about.

Along about fifth grade, when I couldn't seem to learn fractions and I got D's in almost all my classes and I dropped out of Little League baseball because I was so short I had trouble holding the bat—I never got to play, I just sat on the bench—I began to worry if my parents would have still chosen me. If someone had tapped them on the shoulder and said, "Hey, nix on that kid, he's a loser, going to be stupid and short, try that fat little one over there," would they have changed their minds and taken another baby?

I got to worrying about it so much I started pulling at the front of my hair, and pretty soon I had this bald spot about the size of a quarter. You can imagine how that went over! Mom got even more upset than when I kept wetting my bed every night until I was six. She told Dad she thought they should take me to a psychiatrist and he said, "For God's sake, calm down. I'll take him to my barber and have his hair cut so nobody will see the spot. It's just a stage he's going through."

Dad was right. By the time I got to sixth grade and we stopped studying fractions (I still can't do them), and I managed to get my grades up to C's and I joined the soccer team, where speed is more important than size, my hair had grown back—all except for this one spot near my part which is still a little thin—and since I was legally adopted, I decided my parents were stuck with me.

We live in San Francisco and I go to Bishop Alemany High School, a co-ed Catholic high school which likes to think it's a serious college-preparatory-type place, but of course the kids know better. Catholic schools don't have a junior high. You go to grammar school for eight years, graduate, and then go to high school for four years. You can go to any Catholic high school in the city you want, it doesn't matter where you live. It's nice that you get to do the deciding, but it means the kids from your grammar school are going to a bunch of different schools. San Francisco has nine Catholic high schools, and even though BA is the newest and the only co-ed one, only two other kids from my class at St. Edward's go there, Martin Brown and Frankie Gillis. Fortunately, they're both my friends. You'd think, being co-ed and all, everybody would be flocking to BA, but kids pick high schools for lots of different reasons. Some parents insist their kids go to St. Francis to be sure they get into college, and some guys just want to play football, so they head for the school with the best team, and other kids go on to a public school. I guess I picked BA because Frankie and Martin were going there and Mom and Dad thought a co-ed school would give me a more "rounded" education.

BA had a special day at the end of August for all the freshmen to come and sign up for their classes and meet the faculty. Father Harris, the principal, gave us a pep talk about how wonderful the school is and how lucky we were to be there and how he expected great things from our class.

One of Martin's sisters, Maggie, is a junior at BA,

and she was the one who told us to sign up for the Bay Area social concerns class. We were sitting in the Browns' family room the night before sign-up day. Actually, it isn't a real family room; it's their garage. In fact, it still has the garage door. A lot of houses in San Francisco, particularly those that were built in the 1930's, have garages on the ground floor, and the rest of the house is upstairs. Martin told me his father had gotten so tired of listening to four silly, giggling girls that he agreed to turn the garage into a family room if they promised to move the TV and stereo down there. Even though there is now a rug on the floor and paneling on the walls, whenever I'm in that room I always expect to see their station wagon come roaring through the door.

Martin and I were looking over all the papers and junk the school had sent, including a student handbook we were supposed to read. We even had to have our parents sign a form testifying we had actually read the handbook and understood the rules. At the moment, we were trying to decide what classes to take. We didn't have many choices. The only thing for me to decide was whether I wanted Spanish or Latin, and what religion class.

"Listen," Maggie said, "take Bay Area social concerns—Sister Regis teaches it and the class is a joke."

"Who's Sister Regis?" Martin asked.

"You can't miss her," Maggie said. "She's this incredibly old nun who still wears those long dresses and the funny veil. She's so old she can't even remember her own name!"

"What do you mean, she can't remember her own name?" I asked.

"That's nutty," Martin said. "What do the kids call her?"

Maggie gave her brother a disgusted look. "She can't remember her family name, dummy, the one she had before she went into the convent. Don't you remember when all the nuns suddenly went back to using their family name?"

I remembered that. One year our teacher was Sister Scholastica and then when we returned from Christmas vacation she was Sister Joan Murphy.

"Anyway," Maggie continued, "I heard from one of my friends whose aunt is a nun that when they told Sister Regis she could use her old name, she couldn't remember what it was. She said she had been Sister Regis longer than she had been whatever it was and she certainly expected to die Sister Regis and she was sure the Good Lord would know who she was. So"—Maggie looked right at Martin —"my advice is to sign up for her class. You two are going to need all the easy classes you can find."

That's why Frankie, Martin, and I took Bay Area social concerns.

On the first day of school, it didn't take me long to figure out BA is a pretty formal place. The desks in my first two classes—homeroom and English— were in neat rows, with the teacher at the front of the room. But when Martin and I arrived at Bay Area social concerns, we found kids busy moving all the desks around. In the middle of the confusion was this woman wearing a strange outfit that looked as if she'd thrown on a couple of different-colored blouses. Her skirts—she had on more than one of those, too— went almost to the ground, and when she turned quickly, you could see she was wearing sandals that laced halfway up her legs. Her hair had started out being pinned up, but now it was falling down around her face.

"Who is that?" I whispered to this huge guy who was standing next to me.

"The teacher."

"The teacher?" I repeated. I couldn't imagine BA hiring her. With the shortage of priests and nuns, the Catholic schools have hired a lot of regular teachers, but I had never seen one who was dressed as crazy as this one.

"I thought this was Sister Regis's class," I said, looking at the schedule in my hand.

"Haven't you heard?" the giant asked. "She broke her ankle."

"How'd she do that?" Martin asked. "Did she trip over her long dress, or couldn't she see cause her veil got in her eyes?"

"Naw," said this kid. "She fell over a can of tennis balls in the convent."

I burst out laughing. I mean, can't you picture it, this old nun falling over a can of tennis balls? A candle maybe, or a crucifix, or down the church steps, but a can of tennis balls?

The teacher saw us and came over. "I'm Ms. Jackson," she said. "I don't like classrooms where everybody stares at the back of each other's heads. I think we should be able to look at one other. Why don't you help push the desks around so they're in a semicircle."

I wondered what Father Harris would say if he saw one of his carefully arranged classrooms being demolished, but I figured that was Ms. Jackson's problem. Once she had arranged us to her satisfaction, she started to call the roll. She asked us to stand up and tell why we had taken the class and what we hoped to get out of it. I could see it was going to be a class where you're expected to talk a lot. Having a name like Wilson was no help. I had a feeling that by the time she got to the end of the alphabet all the good reasons would be used up. I wasn't very impressed with most of the answers until Rory Walsh was called on; she had sat next to me in homeroom.

"I think learning about the social problems in our community is very important. If we can't fix what's wrong in our community, how can we expect someday to solve worldwide problems?" she said.

"Very nice," Ms. Jackson said. "Barry Wilson?"

When I get rattled, I get silly, so when she called my name I got to my feet, dropped my books, and said, "I needed a religion class and I thought this would be easy."

Everyone laughed. Fortunately, Ms. Jackson had a sense of humor. "I'm glad to see there is one honest soul here," she said. Then she got serious. "I think this can be a very meaningful class. The most important thing we'll do is the class project." She ignored

9

our groaning. "Each of you is to choose some type of public service, volunteer, give oral reports, and write a final paper about your experience."

We all stared at her as if she had announced we were seceding from the Catholic Church. She continued, "There is no text, no homework, no tests, and most of our class time will be spent discussing each other's projects. Are there any questions?"

"I don't understand," said Dan Adams, the giant I had met at the door. "What do you mean by public service?" I suspected from the way he asked the question that he was one of the reasons BA is not strictly a college-prep school.

"Oh, there are lots of things," Ms. Jackson replied. "Helping to clean up the environment, coaching children . . ."

"I'll volunteer for that," Dan shouted. "I'll coach a CYO basketball team for St. Clare's." Some girl leaned across me and whispered to Rory, "He's already doing that."

All of a sudden, the room was full of hand-waving kids screaming for attention. By the time the dust settled, four more boys had volunteered to coach CYO (Catholic Youth Organization) grammar-school teams and Ms. Jackson said that was enough of that, people would have to think of something else. She vetoed baby-sitting but allowed three girls to work at a day-care center, four girls and two guys to help with scouting, and two girls to teach music to developmentally disabled children. Some guy named Jim Palmer wanted to give puppet shows, but he wasn't sure exactly where he would give them. Ms. Jackson said she would let him have until the end of the week—this was Wednesday, don't ask me why we started school on a Wednesday—then, if he couldn't come up with something more definite, she would make him find another project.

"What'll we do?" I whispered to Martin.

Martin shook his head. "Hey, Frankie." He waved his hand to get his attention. "Any ideas?"

Frankie was sitting across from us. He shook his head and pantomimed getting up and leaving.

"Very funny," I muttered. "But we gotta think of something."

Just then, Rory raised her hand. "My mother is the head nurse at Cherry Garden Convalescent Hospital, the kind that has only old people, and she's always saying how lonely they are, some never have any visitors at all. I think it would be a neat project if some of us could each adopt an old person, pretend they're like a grandparent or something, and visit them."

"Perfect!" Ms. Jackson said. "That's a wonderful idea." She consulted her roll book. "Martin Brown, Frank Gillis, Pete Taylor, Rory Walsh, and Barry Wilson. Unless any of you have a better idea, I'll sign you up for the convalescent hospital." She smiled at Rory. "This is exactly the sort of involvement I had in mind. How can I get in touch with your mother, Rory? I'd like to work out the details as soon as possible."

After that class, the day ran steadily downhill. The

locker number they had given me on sign-up day turned out to be wrong and they had run out of lockers in the freshmen section, so they gave me one off in a corner near the seniors. I had my hair rumpled so often and was asked to pick up so many dropped books and was called shrimp and runt and peewee by so many seniors who thought they were heroes or something, I grabbed all my books and took them to intro to algebra, where the teacher informed us that just because we were in the dumb math class it didn't mean we weren't going to work as hard as the smarter students, and to prove it, here was our homework assignment. Homework on our first day of school! I was so surprised by that news I left my books on the desk and had to go back for them, which made me late getting to the cafeteria for lunch. Martin and Frankie tried to save me a place at their table, but some sophomores came over and took the reserved chair away, which meant I had to eat by myself. Eating alone in a school cafeteria makes you feel uptight. I imagined everybody was talking about me and what a nerd I was.

My next class was gym, which wasn't too bad—at least I got to run around and sweat. I felt I could deal with Spanish—the teacher seemed nice—but then I got to history, where we were handed a long outside reading list we would be responsible for. I can't remember when I was so glad to see three o'clock come and I could go home.

Did I mention my mom doesn't work? It's nice in

one way because the house is rarely empty when I get home and there are always cookies and stuff to eat. The bad part is that Mom wants me to sit around with her and tell her everything I did that day. I didn't mind so much when I was little, although even then I didn't tell her everything. Well, you're not going to tell your mother that you got into a fight on the way to school, dropped your homework in the street and a car ran over it and Sister wouldn't accept it because it was all muddy and had tire marks on it.

Just as I feared, Mom was waiting for me in the kitchen. "Tell me, what was it like? Is high school what you expected?"

"Sure, Mom, it's fine."

"How are your classes?" She shoved a plate of brownies in my direction.

"Great." I took a brownie and leaned against the sink.

"Sit down, Barry, you're getting crumbs all over the floor. Are your teachers nice? Is it very different from St. Edward's?"

I sighed and sat down. Mom poured me a glass of milk and herself a cup of coffee.

I ran through the day in my mind. I didn't want to tell her it was lonely there; knowing only two people didn't make for a very exciting social life. I decided she would find the story about Sister Regis pretty funny. I should have known better. Aside from my height—Dad is six foot three inches and Mom is five foot seven inches—I guess the biggest difference in our house is that half the time what I find funny they don't.

"You mean that old nun broke her ankle?" Mom asked. "Really, Barry, I don't think that's very funny. It's a wonder she didn't break her hip. Did they cancel her class?"

"No, they got this really strange-looking teacher."

"What do you mean, strange-looking?"

"Oh, I don't know. She was wearing this funny outfit and she wants us to do some kind of community project. It sounds like an awful lot of work."

"You can't expect high school to be as easy as grammar school. You are going to try hard and keep up with your classes, aren't you, Barry? Bishop Alemany has a reputation for being tough, and you don't want to fall behind at the start."

"Right, Mom." I grabbed an extra brownie, picked up my books, and headed for my room.

"Change your clothes," Mom yelled after me.

After Mom's reaction, I decided not to mention Sister Regis or Ms. Jackson to Dad. When he gets home from work, he usually just grunts at me and settles down to read the paper until it's time to eat. But he likes conversation at the dinner table—I don't know why. Mostly, he doesn't listen very carefully to what you're saying. Let's face it, though, if there are only three people at the table, chances are someone is going to turn to you and ask, "What's new?" which was, of course, what Dad did.

"Tell your father what happened to poor Sister Regis," Mom prompted. "You remember, Bill, that elderly nun we met last February at Bishop Alemany's open house."

When Dad heard the story, he didn't laugh either. He just wondered if the convent was insured for that kind of thing.

"Barry says the new teacher is very interesting."

That wasn't exactly what I had said to Mom, but I let it go.

Dad commented that he hoped this "interesting" teacher knew what she was doing, because it was important I take the right kind of classes if I want to go to college.

I don't know why Dad automatically assumes I'm going to college. Sometimes I think it would be fun to bum around for a while after high school, see the world. Once I had this nutty dream where I met my father in a foreign place and he grabbed me by the hand and said, "I always wanted a son like you." I told you it was a stupid dream.

"You said something about a community project?" Mom seemed determined to keep the conversation going.

"Community project?" Dad's head snapped up. "What kind of class is this?"

"Religion class," I answered. "Bay Area social concerns."

"Seems to me you kids would be better off taking classes that mean something," he said.

Actually, I agreed with Dad, but I didn't want him

to think the only classes I should take were college-prep ones. Since I had finished my dinner, I got up and said I thought it was time I started my homework. That seemed to please him.

▪ 2 ▪

Things move right along at BA, unlike St. Edward's, where the first week of school we had half days and the teachers spent a lot of time reviewing things we had learned the year before. By Friday, Ms. Jackson had our permission slips printed up. They had to be signed by our parents and by the head of wherever we were volunteering and by our counselor. She had also contacted Mrs. Walsh, Rory's mother, who was delighted with her daughter's idea and told Ms. Jackson that on Monday she would have the names of people who she felt would—get this—benefit from interaction with people of a different generation.

It turned out that only four of us would be stuck at Cherry Garden. Pete Taylor discovered Father Franklin, his pastor, needed someone to help run bingo night. I couldn't believe Ms. Jackson allowed him to do it.

When Martin heard about it, he banged his hand on his head. "Why didn't we think of that?" Because it never crossed my mind that bingo could be considered a community project.

"I'd like to get all of the details out of the way right away," Ms. Jackson told the class. "I'm going to make your schedule as simple as possible. You are all expected to volunteer once a week. Of course"—she smiled—"if you want to go more often, that's fine with me."

A few of the kids laughed, but not very hard.

"You will be expected to make seven oral reports and at the end of the semester write a paper analyzing the relevance of your project."

"What does she mean?" Dan whispered.

"It means we have to tell her what we think happened," Martin whispered back.

On Monday, Rory gave Ms. Jackson the list of names. To avoid any arguing, Ms. Jackson explained, she would write the names on slips of paper and have each of us draw one. I felt like a little kid, taking a folded piece of paper. When I opened it, I saw, written out: Alice Pierce, age 83, room 105. Alice! An old lady! Never in my wildest nightmare had I figured on getting an old lady. What did I have to say to an old lady? Well, actually, I didn't have much to say to an old man either, but I don't like talking to girls at all—even Martin's sisters can make my tongue feel as if it had grown a coat of fur. I leaned over and looked at the paper in Martin's hand. Then I looked at Frankie's. Both had men.

"Who'd you get?" I asked Rory.

"Mr. Trent, he's such a dear and so lonely. He

never married and has no one at all. Who'd you get?"

"Alice Pierce."

"Oh, Mom said she was going to put her name in."

"Well, what's she like?"

"It's hard to say. She's sweet, though. You'll enjoy her."

Right. I didn't like the expression on Rory's face or the tone of her voice. I began to get the feeling that this class might turn out to be even worse than I imagined.

Mrs. Walsh had suggested that if it was convenient she would like to see the students the next day, Tuesday, when she would show us around and introduce us to our people. So the next day after school the four of us took the bus to Cherry Garden. Mom had wanted to meet me at school and drive us, but, frankly, I figured the less my mother knew about what I was doing, the less involved I would get. I had decided my whole approach to this assignment would be to go in, talk a little, and get out fast.

I'd never been in a convalescent hospital before, but right from the start I didn't like Cherry Garden. It had a funny smell, a sort of sharp, too-much-bleach-or-something smell, and over that there was this musty, dirty-rag odor that made me want to gag. It looked as if they tried awfully hard to keep it clean, almost too hard. Although the floors were waxed, there were a lot of worn spots on the linoleum. In places, the paint on the cabinets was so rubbed off you could see another color underneath.

While Rory went to find her mother, Martin,

Frankie, and I waited in an enormous room. It had four beat-up couches, some drooping plants, and two or three small tables. An old lady and an old man, both in wheelchairs, were huddled in front of a TV. They didn't look up when the three of us came in, but that was probably because the TV was on so loud they didn't hear us. Even though I tried not to stare, every time I stopped examining my fingernails, I felt my eyeballs zeroing in on them. I couldn't help wondering if the old lady was Miss Pierce. I should have been so lucky.

The three of us sat down on one of the couches. Martin and Frankie kept jabbing each other with their elbows and trying to see who could take over the other guy's foot space without getting stepped on. I pretended I was vitally interested in the sole of my shoe.

"Hey, kid," a voice said. I felt a hand descend on my shoulder. "What's a honey do?"

I looked around the hand to see this bald, chubby man in a faded brown sweater bending over me. "A melon?" I guessed.

"No. Ha-ha-ha," he rasped. "A retired man." The hand on my shoulder shook a little. "All day long, his wife keeps saying, 'Honey, do this. Honey, do that.' Get it?" This was followed by a panting sound I figured was more of his laugh.

"Yeah, sure." I managed to get out a few ha-ha's. "Very good."

"Listen, kid, I got a million more of them. What's black and white and red all over?"

I pretended to think about that one so long he poked me in the arm and said, "A sunburned zebra. Get it, a sunburned zebra."

I moved closer to Frankie, and this guy must have figured I was inviting him to sit down because he came around to the front of the couch. "Who are you waiting to see?" He sat down next to me. It was a good thing it was an oversized couch, but even so, Martin was almost crowded off his end of it. "Your grandfolks here? This sure isn't a place to visit just for fun. Most of the folks here are ga-ga, you know." He made a twirling motion with his hand, one finger pointing at his head. Martin and Frankie stared at him, their mouths wide open.

Fortunately, at this point, Rory and her mother showed up.

"Well, kids," Mrs. Walsh said. "Ready to get to work?" She gently patted the old guy's knee. "Been keeping our volunteers entertained? Mr. Hollis here is our master of ceremonies on amateur night. He organizes the whole thing. We couldn't get along without him."

Mr. Hollis shuffled his feet a bit and made embarrassed noises. I was sorry I hadn't picked his name, but I had the feeling he wasn't one of those that needed interaction with people of a different generation. Probably the only benefit he would get out of it would be to find a new audience for his jokes.

"So you're the kids who are going to try to liven up some of the party poopers, huh?" He struggled to his feet. "You know, kid"—he peered down at me—"when you're too short for sports, it never hurts to know how to tell a good joke."

Martin and Frankie closed their mouths, the three of us struggled to our feet—I think there was something wrong with the springs in that couch—and we followed Rory and her mother down the hall to the nurses' station. Since Rory was familiar with the hospital, she went right off to visit with Mr. Trent.

There was only one chair besides Mrs. Walsh's, so the three of us crowded around her desk while she shuffled a few papers. "Your teacher tells me each of you'll be visiting once a week. Now, let's see, Martin, you have Mr. Wagner." She looked up and smiled. "I think you'll like him. I picked him because, although he has a daughter and grandchildren living in San Francisco who visit him often, he doesn't like being here. I thought if someone other than his family is interested in him he might feel better. At least, it will give him something to talk about when the family visits him."

Mrs. Walsh looked back at her papers and Martin rolled his eyes at me.

"I told Mr. Wagner you were coming, so he's expecting you," Mrs. Walsh continued. "Why don't you run down there—his room is straight ahead. Once I get everyone squared away, I'll come by and see how it's going."

As Martin turned away, she called after him, "Don't mind if he doesn't act glad to see you—that's just his way."

Martin nodded as he walked down the corridor.

"Now then, Frankie." Frankie moved closer to the desk. "Mr. Lewis will love having company. He has no one and he's very lonely. The only problem with him is that he's diabetic and I'm afraid he's not very good about staying on his diet. Don't let him con you into bringing him anything to eat."

"What if he asks me?" Frankie said.

Mrs. Walsh thought a minute. "Just ignore it," she finally suggested. "He knows he shouldn't ask, so I don't think he'll make a fuss. Mr. Lewis's room is right around the corner. I'll check on you in a few minutes." Frankie disappeared around the corner.

"So you must be Barry?" She didn't wait for my answer but pointed to the chair. "Here, why don't you sit down?"

Why did she want me to sit down? Was finding out about Miss Pierce going to take such a long time, or was the information so terrible I wouldn't be able to handle it standing up?

"Miss Pierce is a very old lady," she said.

Since I knew she was eighty-three, I saw no reason to argue with that.

"We thought she might benefit from having someone visit her on a regular basis." Mrs. Walsh sighed. "I'll be perfectly honest with you, Barry. Miss Pierce is very confused. Some days she knows who she is and some days she doesn't."

"Doesn't what?" I asked. I wasn't sure I understood what she was talking about. "Do you mean she has amnesia?"

"No, not really. She knows who she is, but it's as if

she's living in a dream world, and, of course, she doesn't talk much or really care about what's going on."

Of course.

Mrs. Walsh struggled to her feet (I was beginning to think there wasn't a chair in that place anyone could just get out of). "I tell you what, Barry, you go visit Miss Pierce, and if you run into any trouble, I'm always available."

The only running I imagined doing was right out the front door. "But what'll I do?" I asked.

"Oh, just talk to her, try to get her to talk back."

"What'll I talk about?" I begged, but Mrs. Walsh was already going down the hall. I stood up and dug the slip of paper out of my pocket. I don't know why I thought I needed it—I'd already memorized the room number; I could recite it in my sleep.

Condemned man walks his final mile, I thought, as I marched, well, stumbled, toward Miss Pierce's room. Crazed student arrested for breaking down door at Cherry Garden Convalescent Hospital in vain attempt to escape. Or better yet: Bishop Alemany teacher fired for sending students on dangerous assignment. I tried to pull myself together and figure out what I was going to say to an eighty-three-year-old woman who didn't always know who she was. Pardon me, ma'am, no, don't worry, it's okay that you don't recognize me, because you don't know me, and so, let's see, what's new?

All the doors in the hall were slightly ajar, but I didn't look in any of them. I think a bedroom, even in a hospital, is a private place. Room 105 was at the end of the hall, near an emergency exit. I carefully noted that, in case I might need it. I tried the steel bar that was also the handle, and was relieved to see that not only did it move but the door actually opened. Once I was sure the exit door worked, I read the instructions posted next to it, on how to conduct a fire drill.

After that, I decided I should learn how to work the fire extinguisher. I took my time, because I could see that in only a few minutes I was going to run out of things to read. It's like sitting at the breakfast table when you have some crummy job to do such as taking out the garbage, so you start reading cereal boxes and milk cartons. Do you know a half gallon of low-fat milk is not just liquid milk but contains nonfat milk solids, whatever that is, and something else called vitamin A palmitate? I tried looking "palmitate" up in the dictionary (that time, I was putting off cleaning the back yard), but I couldn't find it, so I looked it up in the encyclopedia (it was awfully hot that day, and the yard was a mess). All I could find was "palmetic acid," which is a common fatty acid that can be used in making soap. Well, you never know when that kind of information might come in handy. Just like now I know how to conduct a fire drill and use a fire extinguisher if the need should ever arise.

After a few more minutes of counting the number of acoustical tiles in the ceiling, I finally stuck my head into the room, the same way you finally jump into the water after fiddling around with toes and ankles for half an hour.

God, I didn't know people were that old. I mean,

when I first saw Miss Pierce, all I could think of were those pictures of mummies you see in the *National Geographic* magazine. She looked so old her skin didn't seem to fit anymore. She didn't have any chin as far as I could see, just all this skin that hung down and wobbled every time she took a breath. She had slipped down in the wheelchair, so the only thing keeping her from sliding to the floor was a piece of cloth tied like a seat belt around her waist. Her eyes were closed, and every time she drew in her breath, there was this rattling, rasping sound. It reminded me of those machines in a science-fiction movie when a guy's brain is destroyed by the pulsating noise. I could feel my brain starting to go numb.

"What ever happened to Barry Wilson—rumor has it his brain was destroyed?"

"Didn't you hear, it happened during that project at the convalescent hospital."

I stood very quietly near the door, breathing in short, quiet puffs. Maybe she'd sleep through my whole visit and then I could go away and give some more thought to what I was going to say to her. I had just settled myself comfortably against the wall when Mrs. Walsh came poking in to see how we were getting on.

"I think she's asleep," I whispered.

"Nonsense," Mrs. Walsh said, as she bent over Miss Pierce. "Come now, love." She gave the old lady's shoulder a little shake and then patted her hand. Mrs. Walsh seemed big on physical contact. "See who's here to visit you."

The rattling sound changed to a clicking one, as if something inside her was shifting gears. I found out later it was her false teeth. She shook a little and her mouth quivered. It seemed to take all her strength just to open her eyes.

"This is Barry," Mrs. Walsh shouted. "He's come to pay you a visit." Mrs. Walsh turned and I'll be darned if she didn't pat me on the arm as she went out. It was obvious to me that patting could get to be a habit. "Be sure to talk nice and loud, she's a little deaf."

"Hi," I started to say, and then stopped because the weirdest thing happened. When I first saw Miss Pierce, all I could think was how old she was, but aside from that, she didn't appear to be any different from other elderly ladies. But when I said "Hi," something changed in her face—her expression got softer and dreamier. Then she whispered, "Willie," and cocked her head to one side.

I began to feel hot and sweaty. "Oh, man," I muttered to myself, and thought about that emergency exit. I figured twenty-five steps should get me there.

"Willie," Miss Pierce said more loudly, clasping her hands in front of the blanket. She struggled to sit up a little straighter. "I waited all day in the tower, but then Mama made me come down and get dressed for dinner. I wanted to talk to you—what kept you so long?"

"I'm not Willie, I'm sorry. Were you expecting him?" I said. "My name is Barry Wilson." I started to go over to shake her hand. "I go to Bishop Alemany High School . . ." I never got to say anything else, because when I got close, she grabbed my hand. I swear to God when she looked up at me she almost looked as if she was flirting.

"Tell me about Teresa?" She giggled, and it seemed strange to hear a little-kid giggle coming from that old face. "Were you seeing Teresa? Or were you seeing those nasty boys that Papa doesn't want you to see? Is that why you're so late? Mama was fussing about not knowing where you were, and Papa said she couldn't keep you tied to her apron strings forever." Miss Pierce giggled again. "I won't tell where you really were, Willie, if you promise to tell me all about Teresa—promise, Willie?"

I looked behind me. I had this creepy feeling Willie was there, but there wasn't anybody else in the room. "Yeah, sure," I finally said. What could I do, I felt I had to answer her. I tried to untangle my hand. It wasn't that she was holding on so tight, but her hand felt as if there were a million bones in there and half of them were already broken. I was afraid to pull too hard and break the rest.

I didn't like being that close to her—I mean, the whole thing was spooky. I wondered, if I yelled softly, whether Mrs. Walsh would hear and come to my rescue. I doubted it; she was probably off patting somebody.

"Listen," I said, "I gotta go, but I'll be back to see you again, okay?" I got my hand back and Miss Pierce slumped into the wheelchair and laid her chin on her chest. It was as if I had never been there at all. I backed out of the room, running into the doorjamb. I was halfway down the hall before I realized the reason I was walking so funny was that both my legs were shaking like crazy.

·3·

"Oh, Barry," Mrs. Walsh called as I was passing the nurses' station. "How did it go? It wasn't so bad, now, was it?"

No worse than being eaten by a pack of piranhas, I thought. Naturally I couldn't say that to her, so I just smiled a noncommittal smile.

"Did she talk to you?" Mrs. Walsh continued.

"Well, kinda," I said. "She talked all right, but I don't think she was talking to me. She kept calling me Willie. I guess she thinks I'm her brother. Maybe I shouldn't be bothering her—I could be upsetting her and she might get mad if she finds out I'm not Willie. Don't you have some nice lonely old man I could visit? Somebody like that Mr. Hollis?"

"I'm sure you're doing just fine, Barry. The first time is always the hardest. You'll see, next time will be better."

I wondered if I could drop the class. That seemed the only way I could get out of visiting Miss Pierce. Trouble is, at BA you cannot casually drop a class.

When Martin and I read the student handbook, we couldn't believe what you had to go through to change your schedule. You have to get your parents to sign a request form and the teacher has to okay it and your advisor has to approve it and there has to be place in another acceptable class for you to transfer into. I could imagine the conversation at home if I presented my parents with a drop form.

"Is this the class with the strange teacher?"

"Yes, but it's not the teacher."

"What's the problem, then?"

"Well, this old lady thinks I'm her brother."

"I don't see how that's any great problem."

"It makes me very uncomfortable."

"Son, there will be a lot of things in life that make you uncomfortable. It's just something you have to get used to."

Thank you, Dad. No, I decided it definitely would not be a good idea to present a drop form at home.

"Don't worry about it, Barry," Mrs. Walsh said. "Remember I'm here if you need any help."

Martin came up then, and we both said goodbye and headed for the front door.

"You look funny," he said. "This place already getting to you?"

"You can't believe how crazy that old lady is," I whispered. "Let me tell you that was the worst hour I ever spent."

"We were only there about twenty minutes."

"Whatever," I replied, taking great draughts of fresh air once we were outside.

Martin looked as if he was going to say something

else, but then he noticed his bus coming. "Sorry I can't walk home with you. I have a dentist appointment."

I waited by the front door for Frankie to come out. He was actually escorted to the door by Mr. Lewis, who was this neat-looking guy dressed in plaid pants and white shoes. He opened the door for Frankie. "You won't forget, now, will you?" He clutched at Frankie's sleeve.

"No, sir," Frankie replied. "Two pounds of peanut brittle."

"Not so loud." Mr. Lewis looked over his shoulder. "Somebody might hear you."

"Two pounds of peanut brittle," Frankie whispered.

Mr. Lewis closed the door and Frankie winked at me. "That's the closest I could come to ignoring him," he said. "Do you think it's too late to pull out?"

"I already thought of that," I said. "What reason would you use to convince Ms. Jackson to let you out of the class? Besides, what are you complaining about? He looked like a pretty nice guy."

"Yeah, he's all right, I guess, but it's hard to talk to him, and boring besides. All he wants to do is tell me how hard he worked when he was a kid and how he battled snowdrifts ten feet high."

"At least he talks and makes sense," I pointed out. "You ought to see the nut I have."

"Yeah, well, this is still a dumb assignment," Frankie muttered.

We walked in gloomy silence for a few blocks, and then Frankie turned off. He hadn't even asked me about Miss Pierce, but what did it matter—I didn't know what I would say, anyway. I sure couldn't tell him about that queer moment when she grabbed my hand and seemed to be flirting with me. I walked the few remaining blocks to my house trying to decide how I would describe Miss Pierce to Mom. Maybe she wouldn't be home and I wouldn't have to say anything.

"So, what was the convalescent hospital like?" she asked before I was halfway through the door.

"It was okay."

"Don't be silly—what did you do?"

"Nothing."

"Barry, of course you did something. What was this person like you're supposed to visit? Is it a terrible place? Is Mrs. Walsh nice?"

I decided to sit down for a few minutes to get her off my back. Miss Pierce was nice but a little confused and wanted to sleep a lot. The place seemed all right to me—how was I supposed to know? Mrs. Walsh was also nice and showed us around the place. After that, I escaped to my room and thought about the assignment. The problem as I saw it was to find something to talk about to an old lady. But what can you talk about with an old lady who thinks you're her brother?

. . .

"This should be an interesting class," Ms. Jackson said as she watched the four of us who had been to Cherry Garden walk into the room the next day. "We'll have a first-impression report from those who went to the convalescent hospital. Since I understand St. Clare's basketball practice is tonight, Dan Adams can give his report tomorrow. I'll make up a schedule for the rest of the class so we'll have regular reporting days."

"What's to report? It's only basketball practice," Dan said. "It's the same week after week."

"No, it's not," Ms. Jackson said. "That's the whole point of this assignment. I expect you to report on how team play affects different boys and how different relationships develop. I certainly don't expect a lot of statistics."

Dan slouched in his seat and used a word we're not allowed to use at BA, at least not where anyone can hear us, under the pain of severe reprimand (student handbook). "This is worse than that assignment of yours," he whispered to me.

I didn't bother to answer; I was in a state of shock. I wasn't prepared to make a report that day. I wasn't sure I'd ever be prepared.

"Who'll go first?" Ms. Jackson was using her determinedly cheerful voice that's supposed to make you feel as if what you are doing is a million laughs. I felt Rory owed us one since it was her idea, so I raised my rat-fink paw and said, "Rory knows the most about the operations of the place—I think she should go first."

"Right on," Martin agreed.

Darned if Rory didn't almost leap to her feet, not looking the least bit irked. First she launched into a long, involved account of the history of Cherry Garden. Then she started describing her particular person. After she'd been talking for a while, Frankie leaned over, tapped his watch significantly, and chanted under his breath, "Go, go, go."

By cleverly losing my pencil and retying my shoes at the right time, I managed to get my report put off a day, due to lack of time. Martin and Frankie got caught, though. I don't know what good that did me, except it's easier to get up in front of a class after you hear what the other guys say.

The next day, I mumbled and "you knowed" my way through my report. "Well, I'm Barry Wilson and I, we, you know, go to the Cherry Garden Convalescent Hospital. I guess Rory, Frankie, and Martin told you everything you want to know about the hospital, so I won't repeat any of that stuff."

"No skipping, Barry," Ms. Jackson interrupted. "Each of you has to discuss how the place appeared to you."

I sighed and tried to remember what I had first thought about Cherry Garden. "Well, I guess I think convalescent hospital is a dumb thing to call it. I mean, the people who are there aren't going to get better and go home, or anything like that. Almost all of the people there, like Miss Pierce, the woman I visit, won't be going anywhere else, they're too old. Some of them maybe could live with their families, I guess, like Martin's Mr. Wagner, only he doesn't get along that well with them . . ."

"Hey, don't steal my next report," Martin yelled.

"What do you think a place like that should be called?" Ms. Jackson asked.

I was sorry I had gotten into that. "I don't know,"

I confessed. "I could see where they wouldn't like it to be called an old people's home, but I think convalescent hospital makes it sound as if they're supposed to get better and go home."

"Think about that point, Barry," Ms. Jackson said. "Now get on with the rest of your report."

I described Miss Pierce a little, telling how she had the past and the present confused, but I didn't tell the class that she thought I was Willie. I wasn't going to go through four years known as Silly Willie or Dilly Willie, or whatever other handle some class wit would decide to give me.

That afternoon after school, I decided I'd go back to Cherry Garden since I'd used up all my trivial information on my report. If I was going to have to give another one in two weeks, I thought I'd better see if I couldn't get some kind of a relationship going with Miss Pierce. I asked Martin and Frankie if they wanted to go too, but Martin said once a week was enough for him, and Frankie said he had to help his father out in the family store.

When Mr. Wagner saw me, he shook his head and said, "So you came back, right, but your friend Martin? Where is he? Why should anyone want to visit me? Even my own family just threw me away. I thought you young people were so all fired up on this ecology—yeah—well, how about recycling a few of us old people?" He seemed to like that line, because he repeated it. "I say let's recycle old people."

I glanced over and saw Mrs. Walsh had noticed my arrival, so I figured, what the heck, I'm getting credit for being here, I might as well talk to Mr. Wagner, he makes more sense than Miss Pierce. But Mrs. Walsh, busy, busy, waved me over. Mr. Wagner didn't seem to mind my leaving. He shuffled off, and I could tell he was looking for someone else to grab, to repeat his line about recycling.

"I'm glad I caught you," Mrs. Walsh said. "When you mentioned Miss Pierce was calling you Willie, I went back over her records to see if possibly this brother might be alive, but there was no mention of him. A second cousin is listed as the next of kin. He and his family used to come to see her when she first came here, but I don't think they've been here in over a year."

"What'll I say to her if she keeps calling me Willie?" I asked.

"I wouldn't argue with her. I guess all I can tell you is to go along with her," Mrs. Walsh suggested. "But see if you can't gently lead her into the present."

Now, how was I supposed to do that?

The exit door and the instructions for the fire drill were right where I left them. So was room 105, and so was Miss Pierce. She was still sitting in her wheelchair, and her head was still on her chest. I eased into the room and stood quietly against the wall. I knew Miss Pierce was really asleep this time, because I could hear her snoring. Suddenly she started to gurgle and sputter. She raised her head from her chest and looked around in a dazed way until she saw me.

I decided to start all over again. "Hi," I said. "My name is Barry Wilson."

She giggled. The eyes that stared out of the wrinkled face weren't faded or worn out but shiny and bright. "Is Papa mad? Oh, I'm supposed to say angry—only dogs and animals or crazy people are mad. Is Papa angry at you? He came home early today to take you over to Berkeley to see the university and you weren't home and Mama didn't know where you were and Papa yelled and Mama cried, and whenever Mama cries, you know how Sammy Chang starts to bang around the pots and pans. I bet we eat dog tonight."

I started to laugh. "People don't eat dog," I said.

"Sammy Chang calls it dog, but I know it's really hamburger. Papa doesn't like hamburger. I have a secret—want to hear it?" She looked at me shyly out of the corner of her eyes.

"Sure," I said. "Why not?"

"We have a new laundry girl."

I kept looking at her. There had to be more. I mean, I didn't know anybody who had a laundry girl, but I couldn't see why it would be a secret.

"I showed her your picture."

"What did you do that for?" It struck me as a dumb thing to do.

"Because I like her, her name's Teresa. Isn't that a pretty name? Alice Pierce sounds so plain. She has dark eyes with the longest lashes, and lots of black hair that she can sit on. Do you want to meet her?"

"Why?" I asked.

"You'll like her. She doesn't speak very good English, but she sang me a song in Spanish. Mama made me come away because she says it's not nice to be friendly with the servants. Why?"

I waited to see if she'd answer her own question. When she just sat there looking at me, I mumbled, "I guess you were supposed to be doing something else."

"Where were you today?"

"Oh, you know, nowhere in particular."

"How would I know," she complained. "Mama hardly lets me out of the house unless she or Papa or Sammy Chang take me. Tell me what you did. I thought once you came home from school you'd take me with you, but you're no good at all. At least when you were away you wrote me letters. Now you just hang around those tough kids and make Papa angry. Promise you'll take me out."

She—it was hard to tell if I was talking to Miss Pierce the old lady or Alice the little kid—looked at me and I looked at her.

"Where do you want to go?" I finally asked.

"St. Anthony's Church."

"That's all the way in the Mission District," I protested. At least that's where it was before it burned down a couple of years ago. There had been some talk of rebuilding it, but I think "they," whoever "they" are, decided against it. I was surprised to hear her say St. Anthony's. I had been there once when I was really little for a Christmas program, and as I remembered it, it was a perfectly good church, although it wasn't exactly in the rich part of town. From the way she had been talking, with servants and stuff, I figured she lived in some expensive big house. She was so old, in fact, I wondered if she could have lived on Nob Hill or someplace like that before the fire and earthquake. Now Nob Hill is filled with fancy, expensive hotels.

"Nobody takes me anywhere I want to go," she said, pouting.

"But why St. Anthony's?" I asked.

"Because I've never been in a Catholic church and that's where Teresa goes. She says there are statues and colored windows, and something called holy water you bless yourself with."

"What's so great about Teresa?" I asked.

"I told you, she's nice." Alice sounded angry. "She sits and talks to me, and she's funny. You used to be funny and make me laugh. Are you going to take me?"

"I can't go today, maybe next week." What else could I say? I'm sure Mrs. Walsh would never agree to my just pushing Miss Pierce out the door and over to someplace that doesn't exist anymore.

Alice looked excited. "How will we go? Do you think Papa will let you drive the new car?" She giggled. "I know you can drive, because I saw you from the window. You and that Al Papa doesn't like, sneaking the car out and making Sammy Chang watch for Papa."

I almost laughed. It sounded like fun, learning to drive like that, instead of having to take a bunch of classes and learning rules and then having to watch those movies that are so horrible nobody can eat any lunch afterwards.

"I'd like to go on a streetcar, they make such a nice noise. I asked Mama why we never take a streetcar shopping, and she said when you're crippled like me you can't go on streetcars."

All of a sudden I was sick of the game. I was sick of being somebody I wasn't, and I was sick of pretending this old lady was a little girl. "Don't worry, I'll think of something," I said, because I wanted to leave and I couldn't think of any way out of the conversation.

"Don't forget," she called after me.

If I felt funny the first time I left the place, that day I felt positively rotten. I avoided Mrs. Walsh and just went out the front door. I walked slowly along the street, and you want to know something? I felt sorry for that little kid Alice, even though there wasn't really a kid called Alice, at least not anymore, which shows how creepy this whole thing was getting. The only Alice Pierce was an eighty-three-year-old lady living in Cherry Garden Convalescent Hospital, and I sure as heck wasn't her brother Willie.

· 4 ·

It didn't seem to be starting out to be a very good year. Maybe I had expected too much from high school, I don't know. Since I hadn't felt any different when I graduated from the eighth grade, why should I think starting high school would make a difference? Deep down, I guess I had hoped I would wake up the first day of school and find I had grown a foot and developed a brain capable of doing the most involved fraction problem.

I had a feeling Mom, and particularly Dad, hoped the same thing. Oh, not that I'd grow a foot, but that I would start doing better in school. Ever since last February when I took the entrance exams to get into BA and barely passed, Dad had been acting as if I couldn't waste a minute—if I didn't start getting A's immediately, I'd never be able to get into college.

I heard Mom tell him once that maybe I was a late bloomer. It was nice of Mom to come to my defense, but I wished she'd used another term. "Late bloomer" made me sound like some kind of confused plant that had its seasons mixed up.

I guess Dad agreed with her, because later he said he didn't want to pressure me or anything, he just wanted to make sure I understood how important education is. He offered to help me with my math, but Dad isn't long on patience. He even yells at Mom when she fouls up the bank statement. So I said thanks anyway, I hadn't flunked anything yet. Which, I guess, was the wrong thing to say, because he made a crack about how, if I read fewer comic books, maybe I would have time to do my homework properly. It didn't do any good to tell him that if he'd saved his comic books when he was a kid he would have a fortune now.

I was getting the feeling my life was becoming a repeat of the fifth grade and any minute now my math teacher would assign fractions and I'd really be sunk. I knew I wasn't making any progress when Martin told me he had to shave once a week (the only hair I had to shave was on my head). When his mother offered me all of his old clothes because he had grown four inches during the summer, I thought I'd puke.

So you see I didn't need some balmy old lady who thought I was someone I wasn't and who expected me to take her around a city that didn't exist any-more—all for three units in a religion class which probably wouldn't count if and when I went to college.

Ms. Jackson acted as if not giving us formal home-work was some fantastic favor. I don't know when she thought we made up all those oral reports, in our sleep? Even though most of us in the class had given only one report, it was obvious, from the hemming and hawing, that those reports were not going to be easy. For example, unless I was prepared to report my conversations with Miss Pierce word for word, I had nothing at all for my second report.

Then, on the day I was supposed to visit Miss Pierce, Rory got this crazy idea.

"Ms. Jackson." Rory raised her hand. "I was thinking. Could we plan some kind of entertainment at Cherry Garden?"

Ms. Jackson looked confused. "You mean the four of you want to entertain?"

"Actually, I was thinking of something more," Rory replied. "Maybe the school band."

Why anyone would want our school band was beyond me—it is barely functional.

"Why don't we talk about it later," Ms. Jackson said. "I think Thanksgiving or Christmas would be a more appropriate time."

"But don't you see," Rory argued, "everybody shows up then, it's practically wall-to-wall people. It's now when nobody goes there."

"But even if I could get Father Harris to agree to let the band go, who else would entertain? There are only four of you."

"Yes, and we are a singularly untalented four," Martin said. Then he added under his breath, "If we were talented, we wouldn't be stuck there."

"Speak for yourself," Rory said. "What I want to

know is whether, if I can find some entertainment, could it be part of our project?"

"I suppose so." Ms. Jackson obviously wanted to get on with the oral reports.

"I'll entertain them," shouted Jim Palmer. Poor Jim, he had managed to find enough places to convince Ms. Jackson to okay his giving puppet shows, but he still didn't have enough to make seven reports.

The more I thought about it, the more I liked the idea. It would be much easier to make a report about a group activity than about my one-to-one visits with Miss Pierce. In fact, I liked the idea so much I decided to help Rory out, so during our class break I made a quick trip to the library to see if there were any books on how to entertain old people.

I guess I shouldn't have been surprised to find that the library was weak on books about old people. The visit wasn't a total waste, though, because I ran into Dan Adams. I won't bore you with the absurdity of finding Dan in the library, but there he was, trying to take out a book called *Aggressive Behavior and Its Significance in the Preadolescent Boy.* Sister Nora, the librarian, was telling him Bill O'Brian had already checked it out and two more boys had their names on the waiting list and why was the book so popular since it had been on the shelf for three years and nobody before had been the least bit interested in it?

Dan muttered something and started to leave the library, almost running me over with all of his two hundred and ten pounds. He steadied me with one of his paws.

"Tell me, Wilson," he said. "How can I go on, making report after report, week after week, month after month"—his voice started to crack—"about the practice of some dumb little fifth-graders who can't tell the foul line from the key?"

Since I could see he didn't really expect an answer, I didn't remind him that we had to do only seven reports. He just wandered out of the library and down the hall.

But there was something about old people and his line about basketball games that clicked in my mind. If Rory wanted to entertain old people, how about taking them to one of the CYO basketball games?

The possibility of reports suddenly seemed endless. We, the Cherry Gardeners, could do one on old people and sports; they, the basketball coaches, could do one on the increased enthusiasm of the players when there were large audiences. We could do one on the elderly visiting young people in the community; they could do one on the need for the child to relate to a grandparent figure.

I staggered into math, my brain so stuffed with ideas I could barely lower my head and open my book. If you're not good in a subject, a lowered head is the only attitude to take, unless you like being made a fool of by being called on when you don't understand one word that is being said.

I could hardly wait for class to be over so I could find Rory and talk to her. Mom keeps telling her friends I haven't discovered girls yet. Can't you just see the scene? You're walking along minding your own business and all of a sudden you trip and wow, look what you've discovered, could it be; yes, a girl. Crud. I know girls are there and I can tell a stacked one from a dog. I just don't feel comfortable yet talking to them. I bet three-fourths of them are taller than I am, and if you're talking to a girl and staring somewhere between her stomach and her collarbone, conversation gets a bit sticky. Besides, can't you just feature this: I'm taking a girl out, but since I'm not old enough to drive, guess who's driving us. Right, my father. And what's he talking about up there in the front seat? Telling us the importance of college and how being thrifty, clean, and ambitious is the way to get ahead. Forget it.

I was so excited about my idea I felt I had to tell Rory about it immediately. Since we didn't have any afternoon classes together, the only place I would see her that day was in the cafeteria during lunch period. You would think in a co-ed school everybody would eat together, but even though it's not a rule or anything, boys, girls, and those who are dating all eat in different sections.

When I saw her in the cafeteria over in the girls' section, I tried gesturing and nodding at her, but all that got me was a lot of giggles and some very suspicious looks from the girls at her table. "Hey, Barry, why don't you send up smoke signals?" one of the guys at my table asked.

Finally, I marched over to the girls' section and dragged Rory, well, not literally, over to the side of the cafeteria and told her my idea.

"Wow, Barry, I'm really impressed. That sounds great. I'll ask my mother if she thinks we could do it. Hey, Barry"—she grabbed my arm as I started to back into the boys' section— "I'm really enjoying this, aren't you?"

"Sure," I said, trying to get my arm back.

. . .

I was in a pretty good mood that afternoon when I showed up at Cherry Garden. Mrs. Walsh motioned me to stop as I went by the nurses' station. "She asked for you," she said. "She wanted to know when you were coming."

"She asked for me?" I exclaimed. "For me—Barry?"

"No, I'm sorry, it was Willie she asked for, but that's better than not talking at all. I told her you'd be by this afternoon, and she's waiting for you."

"Terrific," I said. I almost expected to see her sitting in her wheelchair with her hat and coat on, all ready to go to St. Anthony's. I was tempted to turn around and go back out the door, but thank God she didn't seem to expect to go anywhere.

When I came near, she took hold of my hand, and then she started to cry, not loud or noisy, but big tears ran down the wrinkles in her cheeks, and one tear hung on her nose. I didn't want to stare, but I couldn't help it. I wondered if maybe, when you get old, you don't feel as much. It certainly would have driven me crazy having that tear hanging off my nose. I was relieved when it finally dropped into her lap.

"Is something the matter?" I asked. "Do you want me to go get Mrs. Walsh?"

48

"Oh, Willie," she said, and while it wasn't her little-girl voice, it wasn't an old-lady voice, either. "It's all so sad, you and the war and dying and . . ." She started to whisper so softly that I had to lean over to catch the last word; it sounded like "the baby." Then she said, "It's not easy to die, is it?" She fumbled around in that nest of clothing and pulled out a wad of tissue. "I wanted to do something, but what could I do?" She looked up at me, so I nodded in agreement that there was nothing she could have done, I guess—I mean, I didn't even know what she was talking about.

"Mama was right—at least, the way she told me it sounded right. You understand, don't you?"

"Sure," I said. "Don't worry." But I was disappointed. I figured it was Willie she was talking about—dying, that is—and I didn't want Willie to die, not yet anyway. It was as if I was just getting to know him, and I wanted to know him better, and if Miss Pierce—Alice—let him die, then he really was dead. She had also said something about a baby. I wondered about that, too.

Miss Pierce blew her nose loudly and tried to bury the tissue again. "I don't want to talk anymore," she said. "Go away."

So I went.

·5·

But leaving didn't stop me from thinking about Willie. I'm not exactly sure why Willie fascinated me. Except, from what Miss Pierce had said, I think perhaps I liked his life a little better than I liked mine. And I really wanted to know what had happened to him. Miss Pierce had said something about a war—maybe there was something more.

"How do you find out about a man?" I asked at the dinner table that night.

"What do you mean?" My father stared at me suspiciously.

"Oh, like when they were born, how they died, who they married, stuff like that."

"Is it a famous person?" Mom asked.

"No, that's the problem. It's nobody important, but he might have died in a war, and I just wondered if there were lists or something." Seeing my father straighten his shoulders preparatory to giving one of his infamous lectures on, I supposed, the frivolity of

50

idle curiosity, I hastily added, "It's a project for school."

"What war?" Dad asked. "World War II, Korea?"

"No," I replied. "If he was alive now, I guess he would be close to ninety."

"Does this have something to do with the convalescent hospital?" Mom asked. "I thought you were visiting an old lady."

"It's a research project," I answered vaguely. I certainly didn't want to have to go into a long explanation about why I wanted to find out about Miss Pierce's brother.

"I guess it would be World War I," my father continued. "I doubt it would be the Spanish-American War. Was he a local person?"

I nodded.

"Perhaps the newspapers printed casualty lists. You could try the periodical room at the library. I think all their old newspapers are on microfilm now—I'm not sure what the setup is." He sounded genuinely sorry he couldn't help me. I remembered the time when I was in sixth grade and I had to build a model of a Spanish mission. Dad drove me over to Mission Dolores so I could see what a mission looked like, then he taught me how to draw the model to scale. For a minute I almost felt like telling him about Willie, but then I went and spoiled things by asking the wrong question. "What year was World War I?"

"What year?" my father shouted. "Do you think wars are fought in a year? My God, no wonder the taxpayers are revolting, and this isn't even a product of the public schools. I tell you, Anna, education is going to hell."

"Now, Bill," my mother said. "Dates are never easy to remember. After all, 1917 was a long time ago."

"But you remembered it," my father pointed out. "There's something radically wrong with this modern education."

When I got to my room, I thought about going to the library and looking up the old newspapers, but then I realized I could be sitting there for years and never find out what I wanted to know. Why, I could go through hundreds of papers and discover the information had never been printed at all. Anyway, I didn't even know if Willie had died in the war. I decided the best thing was to just keep hoping Miss Pierce would drop enough hints for me to learn about him that way.

You know what? I actually started to look forward to seeing her.

. . .

The next time I went to Cherry Garden, Jim Palmer came with me. "I sure hope Mrs. Walsh agrees to letting me give a puppet show there," he said. "What's this place like?"

"You get used to it," I replied.

At the front door, Jim grabbed me by the arm. "Stick with me, buddy, okay?"

"Yeah, sure."

Mrs. Walsh liked Jim's plan. "I never realized that you kids would make such a difference. Puppet shows and basketball games! Rory mentioned something about taking some of the more active people to one. The only problem with that idea will be the transportation. Cherry Garden doesn't have a bus."

I told her I would talk to Dan Adams to see if he could come up with any ideas about the transportation. Then, while Jim stayed at the nurses' station to set up a time for his show, I went off to Miss Pierce's room.

I thought she would be excited when I told her I was going to take her to a puppet show, but she didn't act as if she cared. She sat there twisting her blanket and shivering.

"Do you feel all right?" I asked.

She shook her head. "Mama won't let you take me out anymore because of Teresa. She says you are a disgrace and she's surprised Papa hasn't thrown you out of the house."

"What did I do wrong?" I asked.

"Mama says you should be getting ready for college and calling on Lucy and not spending your time with servants." Miss Pierce looked up at me. "Besides, you said you would take me to St. Anthony's and you didn't. Willie, am I stupid? Mama called me stupid for not knowing."

"Not knowing what?" I asked. I almost grabbed her shoulder to try to make her look at me. I was glad I didn't, though, because she started to moan and shake her head. It was scary.

"Don't do that," I said softly. "I don't think you're stupid."

"Oh, Willie." She started wiping her eyes with the back of her hand. "Why are you ruining everything?"

Suddenly she looked older, sitting there with her head on her chest, not looking at me. Well, not older—I mean, how much older can an eighty-three-year-old lady look—but empty somehow. It made me sad to see her like that.

"It'll be okay," I said. "Please talk to me."

"You're not nice," she said. "None of us are nice." And then she closed her eyes and refused to open them.

I sat for a while and tried to put all the crazy bits and pieces of Miss Pierce's story together. Something had happened, something about Willie and Teresa and a baby and a war. I had a hunch that Teresa and Willie had used Alice in some way that had made her mother mad at her. I wondered what had happened to Teresa and the baby. Mrs. Walsh had said that all she had left were some second cousins, but Willie's baby would have been her nephew or niece.

When Miss Pierce started to snore, I quietly got up and left.

"See you next week," Mrs. Walsh called. "Tell Jim to phone me if he has any questions."

"Sure," I said. I didn't want to worry about a puppet show; I wanted to think about Willie and his baby. Willie's life was beginning to sound like a movie. Rich son comes home from school and falls in love with one of the servants. You had to hand it to him. In spite of family pressure, he did what he wanted.

I was thinking about being like Willie that night

when Dad asked, "How are you doing on that research project?"

"What project?"

"That one about World War I."

"Oh." I had forgotten. "The thing just seemed impractical, you know. I could have been going through newspapers forever."

"You mean you gave up?"

There he was again, right away assuming I was lazy. I thought of Willie going out and seeing the kids he wanted whether his parents liked them or not. I decided Willie wouldn't have taken any of this crud from anybody.

"Listen," I said. I'm not sure where the words came from, but I spoke them very clearly and slowly. "I'm not a moron and I wish you would stop treating me like one. I am perfectly capable of deciding how and when I shall do school assignments." It sounded pretty good in my head before I said it, and it sounded that way when I finished. Then I stood up and with a great deal of dignity (even Napoleon at five foot whatever had dignity) marched to the door.

"Just sit down," my father said.

"Where are you going?" my mother cried.

"Out," I said, and slammed the door.

I guess times have changed. I don't know what Willie did when he went out, but at that point I didn't know what to do. After all, it was a school night and it was dark and not many people were around and any fool knows the streets of San Francisco are not safe for man nor beast. I finally wandered over to Martin's house because I couldn't stand on a street corner forever. Some hophead might think I was waiting for a contact.

"Martin's not home," one of his sisters told me. "He's at choir practice."

I shrugged and walked over a couple of blocks to a coffee shop. I counted the change in my pocket and ordered a Coke. I could see Willie going into the local bar and ordering a beer, but I knew I'd never be able to get away with that. Maybe Mr. Hollis was right—I should learn to tell a good joke.

The waitress was busy talking to the cook in the back. She plunked down my Coke, rang up my money, and never said a word. I was the only person in the place. After I finished the Coke, I walked to the corner drugstore to check out the new comic books. There weren't any. That done, there was nothing left but to go home. Besides, I was missing a TV show that was supposed to be fantastic.

All the way home, I rehearsed what I would say. Most of the conversation depended on what my parents said to me first. To my surprise, they weren't waiting for me but were in the living room watching TV. As I passed by (why take chances?), I saw Dad notice me and start to get out of his chair, but Mom smiled and called, "Good night, Barry." Dad sunk back against the cushions.

"Yeah, good night," I said.

So much for Barry Wilson's wild night on the town. I decided being Willie was going to take practice. I guess I'm not much good at staging a revolt. To be honest, I didn't get a kick out of marching out of the house and slamming the door. It made me feel silly. And I felt just plain uncomfortable stalking around town in the dark. In fact, I almost wished I had kept my mouth shut, stayed home, and watched the TV show, which got great reviews and will probably never be shown again.

·6·

The next Friday was the puppet show, so Martin, Frankie, Rory, and I were all there. Jim had set up his stage in one corner of the dining room. The tables had been moved to one side, with the chairs arranged in the center and space left for wheelchairs. It was kind of overpowering to see all those elderly people gathered together in one spot. I hadn't realized some of them were in even worse shape than Miss Pierce. At least she was always neatly dressed in a bathrobe, and when she wasn't talking she just sat quietly. Some of the people already in the dining room were not only tied into their chairs but also had trays in front of them to keep them from falling forward. A few of them were talking to themselves, and others kept hitting the trays, making a dull, ringing sound.

I wondered if Miss Pierce would remember the puppet show, but when I got to her room, she didn't mention it. Instead, she asked, "Have you ever felt an earthquake, Willie?"

"Sure, lots of times." Well, maybe not lots, but San Francisco has quite a few minor earthquakes.

"Mama says it's not safe," she replied. "I'm scared. The chandelier fell right down on the stairs, and Mama says it was a miracle nobody was killed."

"But it's all over now," I replied.

"I don't like tents," she whimpered as Mrs. Walsh came in to see where we were. "And the milk tastes funny and my clothes are all dirty."

"Oh, dear, I have no idea what she's talking about," Mrs. Walsh said. "Do you?"

I said I had a pretty good idea. If you have relatives that lived in San Francisco around the turn of the century, you hear plenty about the big fire and earthquake of 1906. One of Mom's aunts remembers having to live in a tent in Golden Gate Park because their house was dynamited to make a firebreak. Even those whose houses were still standing had to cook in the gutter because they couldn't use their stoves until their houses had been inspected. I was sorry Great-Aunt Eunice had moved to Oregon to be with her daughter, it would have been interesting to talk to her. Maybe she had heard of the Pierces, although I know Aunt Eunice didn't live anywhere near Nob Hill.

"Listen," I said, grabbing Miss Pierce's hand. "The puppet show will be a lot of fun, and I'll take care of you."

"Will you really, Willie?" She clung to my hand. "You won't leave me—you'll stay by me every minute?"

"Every minute," I promised and, don't laugh, I patted her hand.

"I'm really impressed," Mrs. Walsh said. "It's marvelous what you've done for her."

It made me feel good to hear Mrs. Walsh say that, but it wasn't really true. I couldn't see how Miss Pierce was any different now than the first time I saw her. I mean, what good did it do her to relive all her old life?

Jim Palmer had put a lot of time in on his puppet show. He has this stage he can knock down and carry around on his father's pickup truck. His father is a freelance photographer, so he has time to drive him places. The only problem with the show was that it was geared for little kids, and I don't care how old and confused these people were, they weren't particularly entertained by watching Prince Charming kiss Snow White. Although Mr. Hollis was the master of ceremonies and he did the best he could, even he had his limits.

I sat next to Miss Pierce, and she kept reaching for my hand to make sure I was there. Finally, it was easier to let her hold it. I could feel my face getting hot, but what could I do?

Mr. Lewis kept sneaking peanut brittle when he didn't think anyone was looking. He would reach into his pants pocket and then, quick, pop a piece into his mouth. I don't know where he got it; I don't think Frankie had been stupid enough to give it to him.

Mr. Wagner, as usual, was complaining. "Where'd they find this act? This kid is terrible. What do they think we are, stupid as well as old?" He poked at Martin. "Don't get old, you hear me, it's not worth it." When Martin didn't answer, he poked him again. "Sit up and listen to me."

"Sure," Martin said, and sat up a little straighter.

Mr. Wagner wasn't the only one who was unhappy. People were muttering all around us. I wondered if Rory could hear it. After all, the original idea had been hers. I could see her seated by Mr. Trent, and he looked about in the same shape as Miss Pierce, all hunched up and covered with a bright yellow blanket.

It's funny how clothes can make a girl look different. Rory had on a dress, and I hardly recognized her. All I ever see her in is her BA uniform, a white blouse and navy sweater, and a grungy navy skirt that all the girls wear too short, so that the nuns are constantly sending them home with notes.

Of course, my idea of dressing up is changing my T-shirt, but BA makes us wear a shirt with a collar. That's so they can measure how long our hair is. It's not supposed to be below the shirt collar. Dad asked what I was complaining about—in his day he had to wear a white shirt and a tie. I can't even tie a tie. On the day we had our pictures taken for our eighth-grade graduation, we had to wear a tie. Dad tied it for me in the morning, and then I loosened it just right and got it over my head without undoing it. I must have lent it to a dozen guys before some jerk with a big head loosened it too much and it came undone.

I was glad when the show was finally over. Miss

Pierce seemed to be getting more and more upset. She clung to my hand when I got her back to her room. "I wish Mama would come and tuck me in," she said. I arranged the covers around her the best I could, and when she closed her eyes and looked as if she was falling asleep, I quietly left.

Rory was at the front door when I got there. "Hey, Barry," she said. She was wearing those crazy shoes a lot of girls have that are more sole than shoe. Mom said she wouldn't wear them because she might fall off them. Before, Rory and I had been about the same height, but now I found myself staring at her chin.

"Good show?" she asked.

"I think it would be better for little kids," I said. "I mean, some of the people resented being treated like children."

"I guess you're right." She twisted the belt on her dress. "Say, Barry?"

"Yeah?"

"How's school?"

"School? Like how?"

"What do you think of the Sadie Hawkins Dance?"

I shrugged. "It's okay." I reached for the door handle.

"Say, Barry?"

"Yeah?"

"I wondered if you'd like to go to the dance with me?"

I stared at her. Crud, those stupid girl-ask-boy dances. The girls always want them, so the dogs have a chance of going. One guy told me he had to hide in the bathroom for days.

"Gee, Rory," I said. "You know I don't drive, and the buses aren't very safe at night." It didn't sound very convincing, even to me. Like what's wrong with your parents or a cab?

"Oh, don't worry," Rory said. "My brother, Kevin, and his girl are going, and he said we could go with them. So that's great." She gave a deep sigh and backed down the hall. "See you at school Monday."

"Sure."

How could I forget Rory had a brother, a great brute of a guy who played tackle on the football team? That's what I needed, an older brother—listen, even an older sister—someone who could prepare me for maneuvers like this. I think things would have been easier at home, too—looser—people just coming and going without having to practically publish an itinerary. It would have been nice if the following Friday, which was when the dance was, I could have casually walked out the door. I thought about pretending I was going over to Martin's house, but it would have looked a little fishy, my being all dressed up in school clothes to walk two blocks. Besides, Mom always reads those activity calendars BA sends home, and she goes to parent meetings and open houses, and with my luck she'd be sure to meet Mrs. Walsh. No, it wasn't worth the hassle. It was easier to come out and tell them and let Mom have the fun of letting her friends know that, guess what, little Barry has finally discovered girls.

The news of my first date didn't seem to rock my father much. He grunted and rustled the paper and wanted to know how we would get there and back. I think he mumbled he would drive if he had to, because he didn't want me riding with some fiend who smoked pot and drank beer. Mom gushed in and wanted to know, of all things, what I would wear. Even Dad thought that was a bit much. Mom took it hard that I wouldn't need a suit; no, school clothes were fine; no, Dad, we wouldn't sneak off somewhere, rest easy, Bishop Alemany is even more paranoid than parents. Juniors and seniors are the only ones allowed to bring outsiders (that's how we refer to kids who don't go to BA) to dances, and then they practically have to go bail for them. No one is allowed in the gym without a ticket, and once you're in, you can't leave until the dance is over; yes, sir, how's that for trust?

Now what was worrying me about this date, aside from thinking up things to talk about, were shoes—Rory's—and dancing. Who wants to dance with a girl and spend the whole night not being able to look into her eyes. Of course, the second problem canceled out the first. I can't dance. Not that St. Edward's didn't try. Instead of gym classes, we had dancing all eight years, once a week. The little kids would learn dances that used nursery rhymes. You know the kind of thing—they would pretend to be Humpty Dumpty sitting on a wall, or one of the King's men galloping around. I used to love that dance, particularly if I was one of the Humpty Dumptys; it's not often you

64

get to roll around on the floor and not have somebody yell at you.

In the middle grades we all learned folk dancing, and when we got to eighth grade we were supposed to learn modern social dancing—at least, that's what they called it. I guess "modern" is a relative term, but somehow I don't think of the Charleston as modern. That's what we learned in the eighth grade. Now, I ask you, where can I dance that?

Martin had told me his younger sister, Jennie, who's in the eighth grade this year, said they have a new dancing teacher. The one who had been there all the years I was at St. Edward's got fed up the first week of school when some of the guys started acting goofy, so she walked out of the auditorium and never came back. Now they have this young teacher who wears jeans and has a boyfriend with a beard who waits for her outside on a motorcycle.

"Do you know how to dance?" I asked Martin. "I mean, other than the Charleston?"

It was Saturday morning, and we were painting the benches in St. Edward's school yard. It's not much of a job, only $2.50 an hour, and the pastor only has them redone a couple of times a year, but it's better than nothing. Martin considered the question for a few minutes. "My sister tried to teach me once, but I wasn't really interested," he finally said. "Why?"

"Oh, I'm going to that dance."

Martin digested this bit of information calmly. "I guess I could ask my sister if she'd show me, and then I could show you, unless you'd rather come over to my house and have her show you herself?"

"Would Maggie mind?"

"I was thinking of Jennie," Martin answered. "This new dance teacher they have is pretty sharp."

When we finished with the benches, we went over to Martin's house.

"You want me to teach you to dance?" Jennie giggled at her brother when we found her in their family room.

"No," Martin said. "I want you to show Barry here the steps you're learning at St. Edward's."

"Why?" asked Jennie.

Martin sighed. "Because he's going to a dance and he needs to know. Okay?"

"Are you going to the dance, too?"

"No," Martin replied. "I wasn't asked. Now, will you show him the steps?"

Jennie giggled again and walked over to a stack of records and put one on their stereo. "Now, just watch."

I could have slugged her. Who does this skinny eighth-grader think she is? But before I could open my mouth, the music started pounding and Jennie started gyrating and wiggling and throwing her hips around. I expected to see a spotlight zero in and some dude in a black satin outfit leap into the middle of the room.

"Is that what St. Edward's is teaching?" I asked. "Does Father Kernan know?"

Martin shrugged. "I think she bribed somebody to

take her to a couple of R-rated movies, or maybe she's been over at a friend's house watching too much MTV."

"Just forget it," I said. "No way am I dancing like that."

"Yeah, maybe she's not the right person to teach you," Martin agreed. "She can be a real pain."

"What's the matter? Chicken?" Jennie called after us. "I thought you wanted to learn to dance."

"Some other time," I mumbled. I turned to Martin. "I wonder if there are any books that teach you to dance?"

Martin seemed to have lost interest. Much as he would like to help, he had promised his father he'd mow the lawn. Let me tell you about lawns in San Francisco. Unless you live in a really expensive neighborhood, the average lawn is about the size of a large magazine. That is, if you have a lawn at all. You could chew it short in ten minutes. I didn't blame Martin, though. Who wants to spend all day Saturday learning to dance?

The public library was out of a book called *Dancing Made Easy*. So I went over to our local bookstore, which is run by this bearded guy who fancies himself a poet. The place is always crawling with your basic nonconformists, with long hair and smelly flannel shirts. Mom went in there once and said they certainly burn a funny-smelling incense. I didn't bother to tell her what she really smelled; she worries enough as it is. Anyway, *Dancing Made Easy* was $9.95, so I just stood there trying to read fast. I could have used some paper and a pencil because the book was full of diagrams with little X's showing where a person's feet should be. It's hard to memorize that kind of stuff and keep an eye out for the owner. I was afraid he would make me buy the book. After about forty-five minutes, the poet wandered over and said, "Say, buddy, is there anything I can do to help you?"

Before I could stuff the book back on the shelf, he took it out of my hand. "Listen, kid," he said. "Don't sweat it. There's nothing to learn, just stand there and let the music tell your feet what to do. Go with the flow." He started swaying slowly and moving his arms up and down. It looked pretty good to me, a heck of a lot easier than trying to memorize a zillion X's. "I'll tell you something else, kid." He leaned over and the smell of garlic almost blinded me. "Nobody really knows how to dance. Just fake it, and oh, don't smile."

"Don't smile?"

"Makes it look too easy. Suffer—that impresses everybody."

Suffer, huh? I liked that line.

·7·

I had a dream about Willie that night. We were in a ballroom with a lot of people. He had on a ruffled shirt and the kind of coat guys wear to fancy dances. There was a girl with him. I guess it was Teresa. She was wearing a dress with a full skirt made out of some shiny material. I was there, although I can't remember what I had on. Willie kept introducing me to people. I think Rory was lurking around. At least there was this modern-looking girl who giggled a lot, although Rory doesn't giggle much in real life. Just when Willie was about to introduce me to my real father, there was this terrible scream and this little girl came in waving a crutch, yelling, "He's mine, he's mine, you can't have him."

It was the kind of dream that when you wake up you still feel as if you're in that place. I almost expected to see a ballroom when I passed the living room on the way to the kitchen. It's certainly not hard to figure out what that dream was all about. To tell the truth, I thought I was intelligent enough to have a better dream than that. Dreams are supposed to be complex and subtle, and this was about as subtle as Mr. Hollis. I could see being laughed out of a psychiatrist's office if I tried to make anything profound or meaningful out of it. Oh, one more thing. In the dream, Willie was dancing and he didn't seem to be suffering. In fact, he was smiling.

For the next two days, I tried to tell myself that I could dance, but by Tuesday I couldn't stand it anymore and went downtown (I was too embarrassed to go back to the local bookstore) and bought *Dancing Made Easy*. Then I locked myself in my room, taped my dirty socks to the floor, and practiced moving my feet from sock to sock. Trouble is, Rory's feet should have been there, moving from sock to sock, too. The big thing seemed to be to keep moving, particularly your arms. The advantage to this type of dancing was that nobody could get very close to anyone else, which I figured was a good thing because then it wouldn't be too obvious that Rory, if she wore those shoes, was taller than I am.

Martin apologized for his sister Jennie and said he thought his older sister Maggie might be free on Thursday night and that maybe he could persuade her to give me a few pointers. The only problem was that he was afraid she would charge me. While Jennie is a real pain, Maggie is unbelievably cheap so I said, "Forget it."

Now, Martin's an all-right guy, but even before I tangled with Jennie, I didn't think much of his sisters.

Actually, they made me nervous. Once, when I was over for dinner, his two older sisters kept cutting down this poor guy who'd had the nerve to ask one of them for a date. Honestly, I'd never met the guy and I felt sorry for him. After hearing a few conversations like that, I wasn't surprised Martin never wanted to ask a girl out. Maybe all girls talked about you at the dinner table.

I guess Martin was still worried about me because on Friday morning he brought me a clipping from the newspaper column "Traveling with Teens" (with a name like that, I wouldn't be caught dead reading it) that had diagrams of a few dance steps. The one I liked showed a guy standing in one place, moving one foot back and forth and using his arms as if climbing the rope in gym. That step looked great and there was nothing to remember or forget. I wondered if I could get my ten dollars back on the book.

Mom couldn't leave well enough alone. When I got home from school Friday, there on my bed were new cords, a shirt, and a sweater. I guess I should be glad they weren't knit slacks, but you know what new cords are like—you can hear them a mile away. And if I had to have a new shirt, how about one of those shiny jobs that you unbutton down to the navel? Ha, as if I could show up in something like that. Still, that plaid shirt made me look like some teenager on an old TV show—clean, honest, funny, and incredibly dense. I couldn't fool Mom about the shirt and sweater, but I shoved the new pants in a drawer and pulled out an old pair that were the same color. I'd wear the new ones when it didn't matter if I sounded like a bunch of mice eating their way through a cornfield.

Dad said he would drive me over to Rory's house. When we got into the car, he cleared his throat a couple of times and I thought, Surely he's not going to give me a talk on sex or something. But, instead, he smiled. "It won't be so bad," he said. "I remember my first dance. I was so much taller than the girl that by the end of the evening she had a red mark on her forehead from my shirt button."

I wasn't quite sure how I was supposed to take that story, but I guessed I should count my blessings.

"Anyway," he continued, "the first dance is always the hardest." I could relate to that.

When I got out of the car in front of Rory's house, he shoved a twenty-dollar bill in my hand and told me to behave like a gentleman and to enjoy myself.

When Rory's father opened the door, he was wearing a gun. For a second there, as my whole life flashed in front of me, I thought he might be one of those nuts that never let their daughters out of the house. No such luck—he was a policeman and had just gotten off duty.

"Understand my wife knows you," he said, motioning me to sit down. I tried to smile at him and ignore the gun. I wonder now if he was trying to tell me something, leaving his gun on. "So, you go to Bishop Alemany?" he asked.

"Yes, sir," I said. Before the conversation got too

heavy, Rory showed up, and no, she wasn't wearing those God-awful shoes but a real flat pair that made her walk like a duck. Then Kevin shambled in.

I have come to the conclusion I am one of those incredibly naïve people who believe everything they see and hear. Between movies and TV, not to mention books and lack of example at home, I have built up a pretty unrealistic view of family life. I thought brothers and sisters were, well, if not friendly, at least civil to each other. It seemed Rory and her brother only spoke when it was necessary to convey some important piece of information. He wasn't driving her to the dance because it was the only way she could get there—no, he was driving her because if he didn't he would lose his allowance for a month. If I thought he, a senior, was going to speak to me, a freshman, forget it. The mere fact that I was insane enough to take his sister out in public was proof of my mental capacity.

I was glad that when Rory and I got into the back seat of the car to pick up Kevin's date, Rory moved over to the other side. Kevin's date—I think her name was Madeline—turned out to be one of those shrill, overdressed girls who make me feel there's something wrong with me. I kept checking to make sure everything was all together.

Kevin dumped us at the door of the gym and told us he'd pick us up at twelve o'clock sharp and drove off. I didn't ask where they were going, but it was a clear night, no fog, and if they looked, I bet the view was tremendous.

Ever feel like you're standing in a room stark-naked? That's how I felt when Rory and I went out on the dance floor. Listen, I was sure every one of those guys who were lurching and stomping out there was really eyeballing me. Rory wasn't any better, though. Talk about two klutzes. I had the newspaper clipping in my pocket. "Stand on the right foot, move to the left," I mumbled under my breath. For a minute there, I thought we were going to knock each other out. Fortunately, our fists collided before I landed her one on the forehead. It was interesting in a bizarre kind of way; I mean, here were my arms practically knocking out Rory, and there were my feet stuck to the floor. Finally, after exerting an incredible amount of willpower, I managed a little shuffle, nothing terrific, but it showed I could do it. Rory didn't seem to be cooperating at all—just standing there, looking at me. Maybe I was doing something so terribly wrong she didn't want to be associated with me.

"I'm not very good," I said.

"All I know is what I read in a newspaper," Rory confessed.

"September 30?" I asked, and she nodded. Rory was okay—not every girl would admit to not knowing how to dance. We did a little better after that; at least, we stayed out of the way of the other dancers. But dancing is not something you do halfheartedly, and Rory and I just weren't the types that could throw ourselves into it. After we stumbled and lurched around the gym floor a few times and said "Hi" to a few people, Rory seemed just as happy to stand around and sip the lukewarm punch. When we saw the nun who teaches Spanish start in our direction, we moved over to the side and found a couple of folding chairs and played around with scintillating conversation that didn't go anywhere. I knew it had hit rock bottom when Rory asked, "How are you getting on with Miss Pierce?" That's worse than asking "What good books have you read?"

"It's not easy," I said. "She's awfully confused and keeps talking about her brother, Willie." I debated telling her that Miss Pierce thought I was Willie, but then I decided I didn't really know Rory well enough to trust her with something like that. "But her brother sounds like a really neat guy," I went on.

"What do you mean?" Rory asked.

"Oh, I don't know exactly—he seems to be able to do things I'd like to do. If I can believe Miss Pierce, their parents wanted him to act one way but he pretty much did what he liked."

Rory agreed it would be nice to be able to do that.

"I think if I could have met Willie we would have been friends," I said. I then politely questioned her about Mr. Trent, and she said he was a dear but didn't talk very much. She was really glad I had come up with the idea of the basketball game.

"I told Dan your mother liked the idea, and he's supposed to phone her about the transportation."

"We should all get together to decide what our oral reports will be about," Rory said. "We can't all say the same thing."

I agreed.

Getting desperate, I then remarked that I hadn't

known her father was a policeman. She responded by asking if I had any brothers or sisters. I told her I was adopted.

"Really?" asked Rory. "Do you remember your real parents?"

"No, I was just a baby, only a couple of weeks old."

"That must be really strange," Rory said. "Aren't you curious about what they look like, who they are?"

"Naturally," I replied. "But there isn't much I can do about it."

"Listen, Barry," Rory said. "There are organizations now."

"Organizations for what?"

"To help people find their real parents. Everybody has the right to know where they come from."

I just stared at her. Sure I do some daydreaming about who my parents are and what they're like, just the way I dream that some morning I'm going to wake up and find I grew six inches during the night, but I think I could cope better with waking up a giant than I could with opening the door one day and having some man say, "Hello there, son."

"This could be exciting," Rory said. "There was this TV show and these people were traveling all over, fighting with hospitals and stuff, trying to get their records. I think you should look into it—maybe your parents know something."

"I don't know, I'd have to think about it. My folks are pretty nice and I wouldn't want to upset them."

"You wouldn't have to tell them at first," she suggested.

I danced with her again to distract her, but Rory is terribly single-minded. She was still talking about it when the dance was over and we were standing on the sidewalk waiting for Kevin and Madeline. Rory suddenly touched my arm and whispered, "Look across the street."

"At what?" It was midnight, but San Francisco being what it is, there were a fair number of people on the street.

"At that man—see, the one in the overcoat."

"What about him?"

"Can't you see, he's staring at you. I think he looks like you—see? He has the same dark hair."

I looked at Rory in disgust. I mean, for fourteen years I've been walking the streets of San Francisco and, believe me, I've never had any sense my father was following me. Now, that guy across the street didn't look any more like me than I looked like an offensive tackle on BA's football team.

"Come on, Rory," I said. "He's just a guy waiting for the bus."

"Oh, Barry, where's your sense of adventure?"

I was going to say something about saving it for the Bay Area social concerns class when she said, "Look, Barry, over there."

"Not another one!"

"No, no, isn't that Mr. Wagner?"

"Who?"

"You know, Martin's old man at Cherry Garden. What's he doing out here all alone?"

I peered across the street, and sure enough, there

was Mr. Wagner. He seemed tired. He kept leaning against the building until his feet would start to slip and then he would straighten up, and then he would lean and the whole thing would start again.

"I think he's lost," Rory said, going across the street. "Mr. Wagner?" she shouted. "Are you all right?"

Mr. Wagner glared at Rory. "Who sent you—my daughter? Worried, is she?" He made chuckling noises in his throat. "Well, she can just stew in her own juice. I'll bet she's looking for me. Told them I was taking a little walk after dinner. Do them good to worry, never give me a thought. Only come to see me when they want something."

Now, that was an out-and-out lie. Every time you turn around in Cherry Garden, you run into a Wagner.

Rory shook his arm. "Come on, Mr. Wagner, we'll take you back to Cherry Garden."

"I'm not going anywhere," Mr. Wagner said, and promptly sat down on the curb.

"Mr. Wagner, you can't stay here," Rory shouted in his ear.

"Ha!" said Mr. Wagner, and folded his arms.

"I'm going to phone Cherry Garden," Rory said. "You keep an eye on him, and don't let him wander off."

"What if your brother comes?"

"He'll wait."

That I doubted, but since she knows Kevin better than I ever hoped to, I didn't say anything more but watched her go into a twenty-four-hour convenience store. After a minute, I sat down on the curb next to Mr. Wagner and watched for Kevin while Mr. Wagner watched for his relatives. Pretty soon I saw Kevin cruising up the street. I shouted and he made an illegal U-turn and pulled alongside us, barely missing our toes. You know, Kevin struck me as an awful ass, even if he is a football player and more than six feet tall.

"Where's my sister?" he asked, as if I'd do away with her and then sit in the gutter waiting for him to show up. I explained, in a reasonable tone of voice, where she was. He looked at Mr. Wagner, who glared at him.

"Listen, kid, you're on your own," Kevin said, and drove off with a squeal of tires just like in the movies.

· 8 ·

The station wagon from Cherry Garden arrived at the same time as Mr. Wagner's relatives, and following them was a police car. The Wagners panic easily.

"Daddy," his daughter shouted, trying to pull him out of the gutter. "You've been gone for hours. Where have you been?"

"None of your damn business." Mr. Wagner folded his arms and dug his heels harder into the gutter.

"You see, you see"—the daughter turned to the policeman—"I can't do a thing with him. Nobody can. We brought him to our house for dinner. We wanted to give him a night out, and this is what he does."

"I'm sure it's not your fault," one of the cops said. "Old people can be very difficult."

"Who's old?" shouted Mr. Wagner. "What do you know about being old? Damn kids."

At this point the attendants from Cherry Garden—actually, one was the cleaning man and the other was a guard they hired after a couple of kids broke in one night looking for drugs—came over and picked Mr. Wagner up by the elbows.

"Don't hurt him," screamed the daughter. "Be careful."

It reminded me of those pictures you see of protesters who refuse to leave and are carried out bodily. I guess in a way that was what Mr. Wagner was, a protester, except he was protesting old age, and that's admirable but hopeless.

The cop opened the door of the station wagon and the cleaning man and the guard deposited Mr. Wagner in the back seat.

"I'll follow in my car," the daughter said. She turned and looked at Rory. "I do love him," she said, sighing, as she got into her car, "but he's certainly difficult."

So there we were, Rory, the policemen, myself, and two million bystanders, who had gathered to watch the fun.

"Now," said one of the policemen, "how did you two get involved, what are you doing out so late, and let's see your identifications."

After turning over our student-body cards, I explained that we had been at the Bishop Alemany dance and were volunteers at Cherry Garden Convalescent Hospital and recognized Mr. Wagner and so on and so on. While I was explaining all this, I noticed the other cop was talking on the two-way radio in the police car. After a minute, he came out and spoke quietly to the cop questioning us and then he gave us back our student-body cards. One of the cops said to Rory, "So you're Johnny Walsh's kid?"

And that is the story of my first date. I arrived home in a police car. I wanted to take a cab. I had the twenty dollars my father had given me. But no, they insisted we climb into the back seat of the patrol car. The cops thought it was hilarious, taking home the daughter of one of their friends.

I hoped my folks had gone to bed, but as we turned onto my street, there were lights on all over the house. At least the police didn't turn on the siren. Still, a patrol car is a pretty obvious thing. The minute the car stopped, I saw the drapes in the living room twitch and, wow, when my folks realized it was a police car their son was arriving home in, they were out on the sidewalk before the motor stopped dieseling.

"Thank you very much, I had a wonderful time," Rory said.

"It's okay," I said, and climbed out of the car. "Thanks for the ride," I yelled at the policemen over the rather loud discussion they were having with my folks. One of them waved and then turned and said something to Rory. At least I didn't have the hassle of deciding whether to kiss her or anything. I wondered if Kevin was going to get it, coming home without Rory. It would serve him right.

I stood in the living room debating whether I should go to my room and pretend nothing had happened. Then I heard the police-car motor start up.

"Well, dear," my mother asked as she came through the front door, "did you have a good time?"

"Great," I replied. My father started to open his mouth, and Mom shook her head, so I said good night and went off to bed. Well, not really. I sat on the side of the bed for a long time and thought. Other guys go on dates without making total asses of themselves and without being driven home in a police car. I wondered if I was ever going to get the pieces together, if someday somebody was going to admire me the way Alice admired Willie. I finally crawled into bed with the depressing picture of Rory entertaining her lunch table on Monday with the details of going to a dance with Barry Wilson. What I should have said to those cops was, "Get lost. We're taking a cab home."

I went over to Cherry Garden on Saturday because it was easier than sitting around the house and having Mom and Dad either painfully avoid the subject of my first date or kill it with too much conversation.

The whole place was talking about Mr. Wagner's adventure, including Mr. Wagner. The old men were gathered around him, nodding and laughing.

"Lifted me right off the ground," he was saying for, I'm sure, the three hundredth time. "I wasn't going to help him, no siree, I can tell you that. Right off the ground."

"Stupid old man," I heard one lady say.

"Listen, if running away would get me out of here, I'd do it myself," another woman replied.

"Fat chance—all he's done is make them treat us like loonies." The old lady turned and gave me a dirty look. "What are you looking at, sonny, never seen someone who's ninety years old before?"

I mumbled something and continued on my way to Miss Pierce's room. I noticed that the emergency-exit door at the end of the hall now had a sign on it saying an alarm would go off if opened. Did they think the old people would stage a revolt and storm out the back way? I almost wished they would.

Nothing ever seemed to change in Miss Pierce's room. I had the feeling time slithered back and forth and never went anywhere. I guess I will always think of her sitting in that little room in suspended animation waiting for Willie (alias me) to come along.

"Oh, Willie," she said when she saw me. "You look beautiful."

"I do?" I asked, looking down at my jeans, which Mom had been trying to throw out for months.

"You'll tell me about it, won't you, the pretty dresses and the food and everything?"

"Sure," I said. The more Miss Pierce talked about Willie and the better I got to know him, the easier it was to say what I thought Willie would say.

"Mama said if you keep getting asked to debuts she'll talk Papa into getting you your own evening clothes instead of using his old ones. I wish I was going to have a debut."

"You're too little."

"Even so," Alice said, sighing, "it won't matter how old I get, I won't be able to dance. Mama said if I'm good and learn to speak up and smile and not act stupid, maybe I can have a tea. But a tea's not a dance, not with pretty dresses and music."

"I'll see you have music at your tea," I said. I knew

it wouldn't matter what I promised, she wouldn't remember anyway, and if it made her feel good for a few minutes, what difference did it make?

"Have you shown Teresa how you look?" She giggled. "Shall I call for her to come up here and then you can kiss and hug her, and I won't watch."

"Never mind," I said. "I'll see her on my way out."

"Will you bring me a favor like last time?"

I wasn't sure what a favor was, but why not? "Sure," I said.

"It's nice being rich, isn't it?" Alice suddenly said. "And going to nice parties and wearing pretty clothes and having good things to eat? Teresa sometimes takes food from the kitchen home to her family. It's all right, though; it's not stealing. Sammy Chang gives it to her. It's old food—we don't need it anymore." She patted her blanket as if it were a dog. "Do you like Lucy?"

"Lucy?"

"Silly, the girl you're taking to the dance."

"She's all right."

"I hope you don't marry her. I don't like her."

"Why not?"

"She called me names, and she's mean. When she came to tea to see Mama, she called me a cripple."

As corny as this sounds, at that moment I wanted to put my arms around her and hug her. I didn't want to hug the old lady, you understand—I wanted to hug Alice. I hoped Willie hugged her sometimes. I was sure he did, though; he was a nice guy.

"I wish you could take Teresa to a dance—she's

much prettier than Lucy. It's not fair she never has pretty clothes. Mama says Lucy comes from a good family and it would pay you to be nice to her. When I said I didn't like Lucy, Mama got mad at me and said maybe Lucy was right, and that I was to mind my own business and that if you know what's good for you, Willie, you'd be extra-nice to Lucy." Alice grinned. "If you bring me two favors, I'll give one to Teresa."

"Two favors," I promised, and at that point decided I might as well leave. I mean, Miss Pierce expected me to go off to a party and it might confuse her if I hung around. I hoped Willie had a better time at his dance than I had at mine, although Lucy sounded like a real pain and not nearly as nice as Rory.

Who should I meet at the front door just as I was leaving but Mrs. Walsh. I didn't think she'd work on a Saturday. I decided then that I really should find out what her hours were in case I wanted to avoid her.

"Oh, Barry," she said. "I hope your parents weren't upset about your coming home in a police car. Honestly, I didn't think that was funny."

"No, no, it was okay, they understood."

"Kevin felt terrible, not being able to wait, but Madeline's family is very strict. She just couldn't be late getting home."

Sure thing. "It's okay," I repeated, one hand on the door handle. Amazing what some parents will believe.

"Dan Adams called about the basketball game," Mrs. Walsh said.

I nodded. "I told him to phone you about how we would get everybody to the game."

"Yes," said Mrs. Walsh. "I mentioned to him that we didn't have a bus. Perhaps the teacher going with you has a car?"

"The teacher?" I asked. "What teacher?"

"Oh, Barry, didn't I explain? I certainly can't let our people go out with just you kids in charge. You can understand that, can't you?"

"But I don't think we can get a teacher to go." I knew the coaches went on team trips and the science teacher gives a field trip to see the whales off the bay, but I didn't think Ms. Jackson would want to go to see a CYO basketball game. Most teachers only want to go on trips that are their own idea.

"I didn't realize that," Mrs. Walsh said. "I hate to cancel the trip, it's an exciting idea. Would you consider letting someone from Cherry Garden go with you?"

"I guess so," I said. Was it possible for kids to do anything by themselves, without parents or teachers always there, telling us what we're doing wrong?

"I know, I'll have Ernie the maintenance man go. He won't interfere with your trip, but he'll be there in case anything goes wrong." When I still didn't look enthusiastic, she added, "And he can drive the hospital's station wagon, so that should be a help. Do you think some parents would be willing to help drive?"

I hadn't bothered to talk to Dan about the transportation; I'd hoped he and Mrs. Walsh would make their own arrangements, but unless I wanted this trip to end up being the parents' and Ernie running the whole show and us kids just coming along for the ride, I'd have to talk to Dan fast. "I'll go see Dan right now." I slowly pushed the door handle.

"Fine. Shall I tell Rory you said 'Hi'?"

"Oh, sure." I turned my mouth up into what I hoped was a sincere smile and eased through the door.

·9·

When I got home, I called Dan, but his mother said he was over at St. Clare's holding a special practice. St. Clare's is halfway across town. It was a pain going all the way over there, but I had nothing else to do and I was afraid Mrs. Walsh would get eager and start calling parents.

"My brother could probably drive our station wagon," Dan told me when I finally caught up with him at the gym, surrounded by what looked like two hundred grubby little boys who kept yelling at each other and clawing at Dan's kneecaps. I was glad I didn't volunteer for coaching.

Dan made a swipe at one with a towel he was wearing around his neck, and blew his whistle. "Cool it, guys," he yelled. "Three laps, and no cheating." With a lot of moaning, the kids started loping around the gym.

"If I wasn't desperate, I'd forget the whole idea," Dan said. "It sounded good when you first mentioned it, but geez, getting all those old people out here and then up on the bleachers—and Jim told me they weren't very friendly at his puppet show. On the other hand, how many oral reports can I give about some cruddy basketball practice? Tell you what, Wilson, I'll talk to my brother. Some of his friends have cars. Maybe I can come up with something."

"Mrs. Walsh said we had to have the maintenance man come along, so we've got the hospital's station wagon, for one," I said. "But she was talking about using our parents to drive."

"Crud, not that," Dan said. "My mother's the world's biggest meddler. The greatest day in my life was when she got a job and stopped helping out in the school cafeteria."

I wasn't going to pit his mother against mine, but I heard what he was saying. "Shall I tell Mrs. Walsh you'll take care of the rest of the transportation?" I asked. It was hard to hold his attention. He kept looking around the gym, counting the kids and yelling things like, "Heads up, Murphy. This isn't the B-league."

"Yeah, sure," he finally said. "There must be a lot of guys I can use. Are we going to have trouble with these people? I mean, they're not going to have strokes or anything?"

"Who knows," I muttered. I was sore. It seemed to me he wasn't doing much of the work and was leaving a lot to chance, and since Mrs. Walsh seemed to think I was in on it, I could get left holding the bag. Actually, I was sure Mrs. Walsh wouldn't let anyone go who wasn't in good shape.

At lunch on Monday, I was relieved to see Rory eating with her friends. I had been afraid she might get the idea that the two of us should eat together. I wasn't sure how seriously a girl took one date. Nobody at her table was looking at me, so I decided she hadn't been amusing everyone with an account of our disastrous evening.

After school, I phoned Mrs. Walsh and told her not to worry, Dan was taking care of everything. I didn't want to go all the way over to Cherry Garden to talk to her, because, in spite of how this sounds, I did have another life beyond the hospital, and I had only two days to learn about the campaigns of the Civil War, and quarterly exams were beginning to be used as a threat by the teachers.

I woke up Thursday morning, though, and realized I was due to make a report the next day. So after school I went over to Cherry Garden. On the bulletin board there was a big poster urging everybody to sign up for a morning of professional basketball by St. Clare's championship fifth-grade team—transportation provided. Quite a few people had signed up.

I couldn't imagine how Miss Pierce had heard about it; I didn't think she ever left her room. But the minute I came into the room she looked up and asked, "When are we going?"

"Going where?"

"You're teasing," she said. "Don't tease me, Willie. You promised me, and I want to go."

"It's just a stupid old basketball game, you wouldn't enjoy it, honest."

"That's what everybody always says. How do you

know I wouldn't enjoy it. If the servants can go, why can't I?"

I didn't know what to say. Mrs. Walsh would never let her go. Besides, can't you just imagine Dan's face if he found he had to get Miss Pierce and her wheelchair into his parents' station wagon?

She stared at me with a funny-mean expression on her face. "If you don't let me go, I'll tell Mama."

"Tell her what?" I coaxed.

"You know." She started to pleat her blanket. "I don't even have to have flowers if you don't want, Willie. I'll just sit and be quiet and not say anything. I was just kidding, I won't tell Mama."

I sat for a minute looking at her. She wasn't talking about the basketball game at all. It was somewhere else she wanted to go, somewhere that was a secret from her mother. Maybe it was St. Anthony's. I tried to think of something to say that would keep her talking. "You might get in trouble," I finally said.

"I'm not afraid." Alice pushed her chin forward. "They yelled and Papa locked me in my room and said he didn't care if I ever came out. They said I should have told them what you were going to do. They said I was sneaky and stupid, but I don't care. Oh, Willie, it was worth it, it really was—Teresa was so pretty in that white dress, and you looked so nice, and the priest did too, in that white lacy thing he wore."

She stopped and looked puzzled. "So you did take me, didn't you?" She put out her hand, reaching for me, and I patted her shoulder. She leaned back in the wheelchair and fumbled around in that nest of blankets, and for a crazy moment I thought she might have a picture or paper or something to show me, because I had a feeling what she was talking about was Willie and Teresa getting married. But she just pulled out a tissue and started to shred it in little pieces.

Still, it got me thinking. Maybe there were pictures of Willie and Alice and Teresa and everybody. They were a rich family—surely they could have afforded a camera.

"I wish you had a picture," I said.

"Once we had lots of pictures." I could see by the expression on her face that she was still confused. "But when they brought me here, I don't know where they went. Mama and Papa tried to get rid of the pictures of you—that is, until you went to fight, and then they liked your soldier picture. But I saved lots of pictures. Sammy Chang brought them to me when Papa said to burn them. I used to go through them all the time. You and Teresa and me . . ." There was a pause, and she sighed.

"Was there a picture of the wedding?" I asked.

"Mama said I wasn't to talk about it, not to anyone."

"But why not?" I asked. "I think it's nice there was a wedding. Was there a baby, too?" I tried to slip that in casually.

"Oh, no." She looked upset. "Oh, no. Mama said there wasn't a baby." She suddenly looked at me. "Who told you about a baby?"

"But you said—" I started to argue, and then I

realized Miss Pierce wasn't talking to me as if I were Willie. I should have stopped right there, I know, but I had to find out just one more thing. "Where are the pictures now?" I asked. I tried to keep my voice low so as not to rattle her. I didn't want her to stop thinking I was Willie, because then I would never find out what happened, so I waited quietly to see if she would answer.

"I don't like you," she said. "I don't want to talk to you anymore." Then she closed her eyes and refused to open them.

I stayed in the room for a few minutes, watching Miss Pierce. I hoped I hadn't spoiled everything. I wanted her to keep talking to me and trusting me. When I left, I walked slowly down the hall. Somebody, I was sure, had pictures of the Pierce family. People just don't throw out photographs—at least, they don't in our house. We have piles of them all over the place, and Mom is always saying someday she will sort them out and label them.

Mrs. Walsh wasn't at the nurses' station. I looked in her office and she wasn't there, either. What was there was the filing cabinet from which she had taken Miss Pierce's file when I first talked to her. I remembered she told me Miss Pierce had some cousins who visited occasionally.

Afterwards I wondered why I hadn't just asked Mrs. Walsh for the cousins' address. It certainly would have been easier. But at the time I didn't think it would be too terribly wrong to look up the name and address on my own. While I was convincing myself it was for a good cause, forget the business about the end never justifying the means, I was silently walking toward the cabinet.

I moved fast. Most of the people around there wear those rubber-soled nurses' shoes. They could sneak up and you would never know what hit you. I was afraid to waste any time seeing if I could find out anything about Miss Pierce. With damp fingers, I thumbed through her file, until I saw the address and phone number of somebody called Tony Johnston, listed under "Next of Kin." I wished his name was Pierce. Then I would be positive that it was a relative and not a lawyer or anything, but I couldn't find any other name, so I decided he must be the one. I crammed the file back in the drawer, pushed the drawer closed, and left the office with such a guilty conscience you would have thought I had stolen the collection money from church. Shaken and ready to swear off a life of crime, I went home.

I wasn't exactly sure what I was going to do with the information. I looked up the name in the phone book and it was there all right, but somehow I couldn't quite bring myself to phone. I'm not much in person, but I'm a complete ass on the phone, muttering and backtracking and finally getting silly. At least that's what Martin told me. "I always know it's you," he said. "You laugh so much." That's me, folks, the original laughing nut.

I thought about the address all day Friday. Half the time my idea of going over and talking to Miss Pierce's relatives seemed a good idea, and half the time it seemed the wrong thing to do, especially because I hadn't talked to Mrs. Walsh about it. Then on Saturday morning I got on the bus and went. That's the way I do things.

When this man opened the door, I said, "Hi there, sir, I'm a friend of Miss Pierce." After I said that, I decided maybe I needed more of an explanation, so I started again. "My name is Barry Wilson and I go to Bishop Alemany High School, and volunteering at Cherry Garden Convalescent Hospital is part of my Bay Area social concerns class." I hoped he thought it was a sociology class. I was afraid if I told him it was a religion class he might be turned off. Some people are funny about religion.

He kept looking at me, so I plunged on. "Miss Pierce is the one I'm supposed to visit." It was hard to think with that guy staring at me. "She keeps talking about her family, and I thought if maybe I sort of knew more about her it might be easier to talk to her, you know?" I could see he didn't know. Maybe he thought I was just nosy. Actually, I guess I was being nosy, but I wasn't going to blackmail him or anything.

"Who's at the door?" a woman's voice came from the back of the house.

"Some kid who says he knows Aunt Alice."

"I really do." I tried to sound sincere.

"All right," the guy said, and then he closed the door and left me standing outside. I guess times are really bad and you can't trust anybody, but I mean, I looked very respectable. I'm neat and clean and heck, my hair is shorter than his.

I fidgeted around trying to decide if he was coming back or if I had been dismissed. I was about to leave when the door opened again and he told me to come in. He didn't apologize or anything, just said, "My wife says she knows about the school project, so I guess you're okay." By this time, I could hardly remember what it was I came about. The picture of some kids on the mantel reminded me that what I hoped to get were photographs. Of course, if he could tell me something about Willie and Alice, I wouldn't object.

"Is she complaining that we never come to see her?" he asked.

"No, nothing like that. To be honest, I don't even think she remembers you at all." I worried that maybe I shouldn't have said that, he might get mad, think I was criticizing him. "I mean, she doesn't seem to recognize anybody." I sat back in the chair, trying to look relaxed, in charge of things, and not like a kid. But then I wondered if I looked too cool—some adults get really turned off if you look too cool—and added, "She thinks I'm somebody named Willie. I think Willie was her brother. I just thought it would be easier to talk to her if I knew more about Willie."

"I don't know what to say to you," Mr. Johnston said. "Miss Pierce was my father's first cousin, so I don't know if that makes me her second cousin or first cousin once-removed. My father always said she was the rich side of the family and if we were nice to her maybe we'd be in her will, but from the way she lived I doubt if there is much money left. Of course, that's not the only reason I go visit her." He looked uncomfortable. "Listen, let me ask my wife if she knows anything about this Willie. She's more up on family-type stuff than I am."

While he was finding his wife, I glanced around the room. He had three kids—at least, there were three in the picture on the mantel. I couldn't see that any of them looked like Miss Pierce, but, as the man said, they could be second cousins.

The wife was nicer than her husband. She acted interested. "How is the poor thing?" she asked. "It's so hard to visit her, she has no idea who I am. My husband says she thinks you're Willie—how sad. Willie must be dead at least sixty years. Don't we have a picture of him around somewhere, Tony?"

Tony grunted. I wasn't sure whether it was an affirmative or negative grunt, but then he said, "Yeah, somewhere with all that junk we pulled out of her house, I guess there were some pictures." He heaved himself out of his chair and went off.

"Does Miss Pierce have any other relatives?" I asked.

Mrs. Johnston frowned. "No, her mother and Mr. Johnston's parents were related, but since there didn't seem to be any other children, she always acted as if Mr. Johnston was her nephew instead of a cousin. I mean, she always remembered him at Christmas and his birthday when he was little, and until she got so old, she always sent our three children gifts, too. I always felt sorry for her. Poor little thing, she really wasn't all that crippled. I imagine it might have been polio, although I'm not sure, but she acted as if she was so crippled she couldn't leave the house. I blame her parents, although I suppose in those days people didn't know any better. After her parents died, she moved to a smaller house with a housekeeper. Actually, I think the big house was sold for taxes or something. I know it was torn down years ago, which is sad. It had come through the fire and earthquake, and then it was torn down to make a parking lot or supermarket or something."

She paused for a breath and I quickly said, "I understand Willie was married?" before she started talking again.

"Really? I never heard that. I wonder what happened. Maybe his wife died." Mrs. Johnston gave a little laugh. "Of course, she died, but maybe she died very young. Funny Miss Pierce never mentioned her, because she seemed close to Willie and talked about him constantly. She really only trusted family, but with the children and all, it's been hard for us to visit her very often."

I sat back in the chair. I didn't feel as if I had to be quite so careful with the impression I was making on Mrs. Johnston. "Do you think there could have been a baby?"

Mrs. Johnston looked at me. "If there was, I never heard about it. You're not thinking Mr. Johnston would be that baby, are you?"

I sat up straight in the chair. Why, I didn't even like Mr. Johnston—how could he be Willie's baby? "No, no," I assured her, and fortunately at that point Mr. Johnston came back carrying a small carton. "God knows where Willie is in this mess," he said, dropping the box on the floor.

I eyed it hungrily. Dare I suggest that I take it

home? I looked at Mr. and Mrs. Johnston and they looked at me. I was the first to drop my eyes.

"I don't imagine there's anything valuable in there," Mrs. Johnston said. "Why don't you bring the photographs over to Aunt Alice. She might enjoy seeing them. Then if there isn't room to keep them at the hospital, you can return them to us."

I looked at Mr. Johnston, but he just muttered something about it taking up space in the closet and, with the way people in this family kept buying things, there wasn't an inch to spare in the closets anyway.

I almost ran from the room, thanking them at every step. I was afraid they might change their minds before I got to the door. Only when I was safely outside did I realize it wasn't going to be easy to drag that open carton home on the bus. Finally I took my jacket off and stuffed it on the top, so no pictures blew away. Then I staggered off to the bus stop.

·10·

When I got home, there was a note on the refrigerator from my folks telling me they had gone off to play golf but would be home around four. I moved the carton into the living room, made myself a couple of bologna sandwiches, opened a quart of milk, grabbed a dozen cookies, and was ready for a few hours of detective work.

I went through all the pictures slowly and carefully. There was a professional portrait of Alice. She wasn't pretty at all—the best you could say was that she was cute. She had freckles, and her teeth were too big and her face too thin, and there was too much nose. Her hair looked stiff and she held her head as if she was afraid she would spoil the curl.

The rest of the pictures were of adults in long, dark clothes, standing in tight groups. I couldn't find any of a young man. It looked as if Alice had been right—her parents had thrown out the pictures of Willie. But she had said they had saved one of him in his uniform, so I kept looking and at the bottom of the carton, in a large yellow envelope, I found it.

So this was Willie. I held the photograph away from me so I could get a better perspective on it. He looked a little like Alice, thin and freckled, but on him the nose was a better fit. It was impossible to tell from the picture how tall he was—it was a shot of him from the shoulders up—but you could see he had on a uniform. He wasn't smiling, and I wondered if he was hiding the same large front teeth Alice had. Both of them had light, wispy hair. He probably would have been bald by the time he was thirty, I thought, and for some reason that made me feel better.

I put the picture on the coffee table and tried studying it. "Hello, **Willie**," I said. I wanted the picture to say something to **me**, to give me a sense that Willie and I meant something to each other, that we had some kind of connection, but he just sat there looking serious and self-important, very much the big brother.

I heard the car door slam, so I gathered up the pictures and the carton and brought them to my room. I propped up Willie's picture on the bureau. Maybe he was the kind of guy it took a while to get to know.

My folks were planning to go to the movies that night, did I want to go or was I taking Rory out, anyway dinner would be at six, would I be there? No to questions 1 and 2, yes to 3, my hands would be washed and I'd be at the table at six.

. . .

On Sunday night, Mrs. Walsh phoned me. For a minute I was scared—suppose the Johnstons had gotten in touch with her. But she just wanted to make sure I was going on the basketball trip because, while she realized that certainly Miss Pierce couldn't go, I was so good with old people she would feel much better if I was along, and if it was any problem, the time I spent at the basketball game would count for a visit. After I hung up, I realized I would have to tell Mrs. Walsh about the Johnstons.

The following Saturday, I was already at Cherry Garden when Dan arrived with his brother. They drove up in a station wagon and were followed by a van. I don't know what he offered his brother and his brother's friend for driving, maybe a life interest in the BA athletic club.

Dan's team wasn't scheduled to play until eleven, but he was anxious to get going, claiming he still had to get his kids organized. I asked him why he hadn't organized them the night before, and he gave me a dirty look and said he could hardly make sure they had their uniforms on the night before, and besides, he wanted to go over their plays one more time.

Ernie and Mrs. Walsh had all the people ready to go. Mr. Wagner was there and Mr. Hollis, who was keeping up everybody's spirits by telling his same old, tired jokes. I was surprised to see the old lady who had crabbed so much at the puppet show, but maybe going to things gave her something to crab about.

"I hope you don't expect me to get into that truck thing," she said. "It looks like a hearse, my word, there are hardly any windows, just those little portholes, and stop shoving," she snapped at Dan, who was trying to help her into the van.

He pulled back, looking scared. "It's a van," he stuttered. "I was only trying to help you."

"I don't care what you call it, I'm not riding in anything that looks like a hearse, time enough for that."

"You tell 'em, Maisie," Mr. Wagner shouted. "Just because we're old, they think they can tell us what to do. Don't listen to them."

Ernie looked at Joey, who was leaning against his van. "Do you have a driver's license, kid?"

"Yeah, sure." Joey looked surprised.

"Let's see it."

Joey dug into his pocket and pulled out his license. Ernie looked at it carefully before he handed it back. "Your van?" he asked.

"Yeah, well, I mean me and my Dad's."

"Got insurance?"

"Sure."

"Drive that black bomb carefully, you hear?" Ernie put his hand firmly under Maisie's elbow and guided her to the hospital's station wagon.

"Right," Joey said.

By the time Ernie and I had gotten everybody arranged, Frankie and Martin and Rory showed up. Where were they when I needed them? Dan was no help at all. After Maisie, he acted as if he was afraid of touching anyone. He hung around the van and kept saying, "This'll never work."

Frankie and Martin didn't want to ride in the van

either. "He's a wild man," Martin said, looking over at Joey. "You know that hedge that disappeared at BA, well, that's him. His father tried to take away his license, but his mother got it back for him. No way am I going to ride with that nut."

I hoped Ernie hadn't heard that. "Hey, Dan," I yelled. "You have to ride in the van."

Dan looked startled. "Why? I was going to ride with my brother."

"They need you in the van."

"Oh," Dan said and quietly got into the van. I was amazed how easy it was to control him, I mean, he's so much bigger than I am. I hoped having Dan in the van with me might keep Joey driving at less than suicidal speed. He kept assuring me that Joey was really driving in a very sane manner, for him, but the residents of Cherry Garden had to keep grabbing on to the side of van every time he took a turn too fast.

As soon as we got to the gym, Dan leaped out and said, "Have to see to my kids," and, with his brother, disappeared. Joey pulled his cap over his eyes and slouched down behind the wheel, making it obvious he was going nowhere. I gathered up the hats (all old ladies seem to wear hats), umbrellas (it didn't look like rain), mufflers (it was 65 degrees out), and coats and purses.

We were almost an hour early for Dan's team, but the trouble is the CYO schedules games all morning, so, as we entered the gym, we were confronted with a bunch of third-graders slugging it out. There we were, the five of us, counting Ernie, who was hanging back, and fifteen old people and a gym full of bloodthirsty third-graders and howling parents and two referees blowing whistles and running up and down the court and various people checking clocks and keeping score.

"I think," Maisie said in a very loud, clear voice, "I want to go back to my room now."

One of the coaches hustled over and suggested that maybe we had come to the wrong place, that the community room was on the other side of the church and this was a basketball game, and we just couldn't have all those people standing near the door, it wasn't safe, and besides, it was against the fire law.

Rory and I agreed that yes, it certainly was a basketball game and that was what we had come to see, and if somebody could call a time-out, we would be glad to sit down. Apparently, this wasn't a decision he could make alone, because he went over to confer with the other coach, the referee, and the score-keeper. Finally, somebody blew a whistle and the third-graders stopped running up and down the court like maniacs.

"Hurry up," yelled the referee. "We have five games scheduled this morning and we're already behind."

Then Maisie pointed out, quite accurately, that one of them could be hit by a ball. "She's right," I said to Rory. "Those basketballs are all over the place."

We—Rory, Martin, Frankie, and I (Ernie hadn't said anything)—decided half court was probably the safest place to be. That would put us an equal distance from each basket, away from most of the action. We got some of the more agile old men up on the second and third steps of the bleachers, and arranged the others on the first step, with the four of us sitting between them. Satisfied we had everything under control, Ernie said, "I'm going outside for a smoke. Mrs. Walsh said you kids were in charge. If you need me, I'll be by the snack bar."

We barely nodded at him, we were so busy watching the ball. If it seemed to be heading for our group, we decided we would throw ourselves in its path. I know it sounds crazy, writing about it now, but by then we were desperate. If Martin had asked one more time whose dumb idea this was, I think I would have found a basketball and hit him with it.

I suppose it would have meant more if they knew the kids or knew the coach or knew somebody. A few of the men were able to follow the game pretty well, and the ladies tried to be pleasant and cheered everybody. There was one near-miss with the ball, but it stopped the game because Maisie let out this terrible scream and then kept brushing at her skirt as if the ball had a life of its own and was going to attack her.

When the third-graders' game was over, we got everybody a little better arranged before Dan's team came out. We brought Mr. Wagner down to the first row when he said he had played basketball as a young man. He agreed to help us watch out for balls.

Dan's team didn't win, but it didn't matter because

nobody seemed to be able to keep the kids straight anyway. They both had red-and-white uniforms: the home team (Dan's) had red tops and white bottoms, and the visitors had white tops and red bottoms. I can understand how they'd get confused. When the kids were scrambling all over the floor for the ball, I had trouble keeping track. Of course, basketball was never my game. Whenever Dan looked happy, though, everybody yelled.

During halftime, Martin and I went to the snack bar for some coffee and candy. When we got back, Maisie wanted to know if she could have a nice cup of tea instead, which set off two or three other ladies, who said their doctors wouldn't let them drink coffee but how about a nice glass of ice water? Rory and Frankie drank the leftover coffee. I really can't stand the stuff, maybe because deep down I believe all that junk about it stunting your growth—why take chances? Some of the old people complained about the choice of candy, too, but I noticed it all got eaten.

When the game was finished, Dan came over and said since some of the kids didn't have rides home he would have to wait around until his father showed up in his car so they could drive the kids home. When I made growling noises, he looked me straight in the eye and said, "My first responsibility is to the kids. I can't leave them, and this was a pretty stupid idea if you ask me."

"Just make sure your brother and Joey are outside," I snarled. Dan looked a little startled at my tone of voice, but he said, "Yeah, sure, right away, no hard feelings, huh?"

When we were all assembled outside, Ernie leaned into the van, where Joey appeared to be asleep. "Thirty-five," he said. "One mile over and I'll report you to the police for reckless driving."

"Okay," Joey said, pushing his cap back on his head.

Rory rode in the van going home. I have to admit she's really good with old people. She gets them laughing and kidding and pretty soon they stop complaining. I think maybe I get too serious. I run around and try to be pleasant and not hurt anyone's feelings, and the whole thing gets to be a mess. Rory had them all singing songs and seeing who could tell the silliest joke, and after a while even Joey broke into a song as he careened around the corners.

When we dropped the group off at Cherry Garden, everybody thanked us for a really nice morning and said they hoped they could do it again. By this time, I was feeling so great about everything and Rory looked so cute standing there patting Mr. Wagner's hand that I asked her if she'd like to go to the movies Sunday afternoon. I would have preferred going at night—it would be more like a real date that way—but without a car it's not easy getting around.

"Sure, Barry, I'd love to," she said.

And that shows what a really neat kid she is, because she didn't even ask me what movie we were going to see or anything. It made me feel good that she trusted me to pick it out. I wondered if I should ask her to dinner afterwards but decided not to overdo it. I could save that for a third date—that is, if there was going to be a third date.

·11·

I wasn't in a hurry to get the pictures over to Miss Pierce. I found I enjoyed going over them. I decided they must have been a strange family. Most people have tons of pictures of their children and hardly any of themselves, but in the Pierces' case you'd hardly know there had been any children at all.

Finally, I packed all the pictures in two shoe boxes and brought them to Cherry Garden. Before I went to Miss Pierce's room, I stopped by the nurses' station. "I hope you don't mind, Mrs. Walsh," I said. My heart was banging so hard I was afraid she would ask me what's wrong. "I went to see Miss Pierce's cousin."

"Why, Barry, how nice of you. I'm sure they appreciated your being so concerned about Miss Pierce that you'd want to visit them."

I just stared at her.

"How did you find their address?"

"I looked it up in the phone book." I had, after I

had found their name in the file cabinet. I hoped Mrs. Walsh wouldn't remember she had never mentioned their name to me.

"You didn't go to too much trouble, did you, because I would have been glad to have given it to you."

I couldn't believe I'd worked myself into such a panic over something she was treating so casually. "Anyway," I said, "they gave me these photographs they thought Miss Pierce might enjoy."

"Wonderful," Mrs. Walsh said. "I'm sure she'll love looking at them."

She didn't. "Silly things," she said, letting a few drop to the floor. "Mama burnt all the nice ones."

"I thought there might be one of Teresa," I said.

"Why?" she asked. "She's dead. Mama said she died of the flu—everybody was sick then. I had to stay in my room and the nurse hung sheets on the window that smelled funny. It didn't matter, though—she wasn't washing for us anymore anyway."

"But I thought she and Willie were married."

She stared at me with blank eyes. "You mustn't ever say that," she said. "Mama would get very angry if she heard that." She closed her eyes and refused to talk anymore.

I gathered up the pictures, put them back in the shoe boxes, and left them on her bedside table. I hoped that, after I left, she would get curious and look at them. It was only when I got outside that I realized she hadn't called me Willie.

. . .

It began to look as if I was never going to find out anything more about Willie and Teresa. I figured the

112

only ones left alive were Miss Pierce and the baby. I wondered what had happened to the baby. Had Miss Pierce raised the baby and was that why she never left the house? Somehow that didn't fit in with what I had found out about her life so far. Besides, the Johnstons had never heard of any baby, unless Tony Johnston was the baby and they didn't want anybody to know. But he was such a slob!

It was too bad St. Anthony's had burnt down. Maybe they had records of marriages and baptisms. I felt as if the strings of the puzzle were at my fingertips and I just couldn't grab the ends. Then the following Monday Mrs. Johnston phoned me.

"Barry, this is Helen Johnston."

It took me a minute to recognize the name. "Yes?" I asked.

"You remember our conversation about Willie being married and there being a baby? Well, I started going through the things we brought from Aunt Alice's house, really going through, and I found another box of pictures. It was buried under old letters and hair ribbons and handkerchiefs—things like that. I'm surprised we didn't throw it out as junk, we have so little storage space . . ."

I let her rattle on because I was trying to decide what to say. Did I have the right to ask her if I could see the pictures? Suppose she turned me down and told me to stop meddling?

"I haven't had time to go through them, but I thought if you wanted to pick them up, maybe you could bring them over to Aunt Alice. Don't you think Mrs. Walsh is right?"

"Right?" I wondered if I had missed some of the conversation.

"Yes, when Aunt Alice first started getting so confused—why, one day she'd know us and the next day she'd think we were the servants—Mrs. Walsh told us we should try to make her live in the present as much as possible and not let her keep forgetting. So could you pick them up? I thought the pictures might mean more to her if you brought them in."

All of a sudden I felt guilty. I hadn't been trying to make her live in the present at all. I had been playing along with her confusion just because I had gotten curious and wanted to find out what happened to Willie.

I went right over to the Johnston house. It was only 3:45, and I figured Mr. Johnston was still at work. There was nothing really wrong with him, except I didn't like him. Face it, it's hard to like a guy who leaves you standing out on the front steps with the door shut while he decides if you're safe enough to come into his precious home.

"I know we should visit more often." Mrs. Johnston kept making apologies, all the while fussing with the box in her hand. I waited as patiently as I could, and when she finally handed it over, I said, "I'll take good care of them, don't worry. I left the other pictures with her, but she didn't seem too interested, so I'll return them to you."

"There's no hurry."

By the time I got home, it was dinnertime. It takes forever going on the bus, especially during rush hour. Then dinner dragged on. Dad was in one of his moods when he decides to talk about his time in the Marines. I'm not sure what started him. Even Mom's eyes began to glaze over before we worked our way through boot camp and on to Korea. When he stopped long enough to sip from his coffee cup, I bolted from the kitchen, muttering that I had tons of homework to do.

I was so excited my hands were shaking when I opened the box and finally got a real look at Willie and Alice. Miss Pierce had managed to save a lot of pictures. She was always sitting down, and you had to look very closely to see the crutches tucked away in some corner. I guess she didn't like to be seen with them, or maybe her mother didn't want them in the pictures. I can understand that—even Mom takes off her glasses when a camera appears. Just as I suspected, Willie was tall. At least, he was a lot taller than his father. There were a couple of pictures of Willie and his father. They were standing next to each other but not touching. In fact, in all the pictures no one in the family seemed to notice anyone else. It was sad, looking at Alice seated next to this thin woman who must have been her mother, and they weren't even looking at each other. There were a few of Willie and Sammy Chang, and then finally, in a group of the whole household, including two or three women in long, white aprons, there a short, plump girl with long black hair and big sad eyes. Willie was standing close to her, and if you stared at the picture very closely, you could see he actually had his arm around her.

The only other picture of Teresa was one of her

standing in front of a church. She was wearing a dress with lots of ruffles and stuff, and she was holding a bouquet of flowers. There was one of Alice and Teresa together, and I was glad to see Teresa had her arm around Alice. Alice's bouquet of flowers looked exactly like Teresa's. I guessed Willie had taken these pictures, because he wasn't in any of them.

Down in the bottom of the box was a copy of the picture of Willie in his army uniform, this time in a frame. The glass was broken, and when I went to pick out the pieces, the picture looked bulgy, as if something was stuck between the picture and the backing. I carefully slid the picture out and found two folded, yellowed papers. I smoothed them slowly with my fingers, debating whether I should open them. I finally decided why not, how could I help Miss Pierce if I didn't know about everything? I don't have a very strong will, and I can talk myself into anything.

The first piece of paper was a marriage license. William Bradford Pierce, bachelor, married Teresa Vásquez, spinster, on May 31, 1915, St. Anthony's Church. The second piece of paper was a certificate of baptism. Name—William Bradford Pierce III, son of William Bradford Pierce II and Teresa Vásquez, born in San Francisco, California, on the eighteenth day of December 1915. I read that paper over a dozen times. So there was another Willie Pierce. If only I knew where he was.

You would have thought I'd have gone to the

hospital the minute school was out the next day, but, funny as it sounds, I couldn't make myself go. To be honest, I was afraid; it was like the time Rory had suggested I try to find my real parents. I guess I didn't really want to find them because I like to keep pretending they are fantastic. With Willie, I wanted to keep thinking he was special. But even though part of me didn't want to know, part of me did, so on Saturday morning I brought the shoe box over and gave it to Miss Pierce. She looked at me for a moment as if she wasn't sure who I was. She let the box sit on her lap and made no move to open it.

"Unwrap it," I urged.

She fingered the string on the box, and then she smiled a funny half smile and I knew that even if she wasn't calling me Willie, she still thought she was a little girl.

"Have you brought me a present?" she asked. "What is it?"

"Look and see."

She slowly lifted the lid and took out the first picture. It was of the servants and Willie and Teresa on the front lawn.

"Oh," she said, staring at the photograph. Carefully she took the other pictures from the box and examined them one by one. Finally, she came to the marriage license and baptism certificate. I had deliberately put them at the bottom. I held my breath, waiting to hear what she would say.

She giggled softly. "Willie hid these. He told me not to let anyone see them. He had to sneak the baby to the church one night—Teresa made him. He made me promise I wouldn't tell anyone. I'll tell you a terrible secret—Mama gave the baby away."

"What do you mean?" I asked. "How do you know?"

"I know." Alice's voice quivered. "Teresa told me before she left. Mama let her stay until she had the baby. Mama said it was our duty to keep her until then. Besides, I heard Papa say Teresa would have to sign some papers and they would have to keep an eye on her until everything went through."

"But where was Willie? It was his baby, too."

"Oh, Papa sent him off. When he and Mama found out they got married, and then about the baby, they got a judge to say they weren't married at all. But it's not true—I saw the priest marry them."

"Willie just went away?" I couldn't believe it. Not my Willie, not the World War I hero, not Alice's adored big brother? "He just left Teresa?"

She nodded. "But he snuck back one night. Teresa had the baby in her bedroom. That's when he took it to church, cause Teresa was crying so much. But Mama wouldn't let them keep the baby, and she made Willie leave before Papa found out. I'm tired, I don't want to talk anymore."

"What?" I said. "Why didn't Willie take Teresa with him?"

"I'm tired," she said again.

"You can't stop now," I cried. "What happened to the baby?"

"I don't want to talk. Mama said the whole thing was a disgrace and we must never, never talk about it." Her mouth quivered. "Mama said if I ever told anybody she would send me away, too, but you're not anybody, are you?" She looked at me in a confused way, and then she put out her hand and tried to grab mine. "But you're not anybody, are you?" She kept looking at me as if she wasn't sure. "It was all right to tell you, wasn't it?"

"But what happened to the baby?" I repeated. "Did Teresa take it?"

"Oh, no, Mama wouldn't let her. Mama gave the baby to the nuns."

"She just gave the baby away?" I asked. "How could she give a baby away?"

"Mama said we couldn't have a baby like that, and besides Teresa wouldn't care because those kind of people have lots of babies and she'd never miss it and how could Willie marry Lucy if he had a baby?"

I sat down on Miss Pierce's bed. "But Willie wouldn't do that," I said.

"Papa made him."

Since when had Willie done what his father wanted, I thought. And then I realized Willie wouldn't have obeyed his father if he hadn't thought it was right. But how could Willie think it was right? He and Teresa had a real baby, who was going to grow up and become a real person. You don't have a baby and then pretend he doesn't exist.

"What kind of people give babies away?" I suddenly shouted at Miss Pierce.

She started to cry. "Mama said the nuns are good to babies." She huddled in the corner of her wheelchair and began picking at the fuzz on her blanket. "I don't like you."

I stood up to go. All I could think was that they had given Willie's baby away and Willie hadn't cared. He was as bad as my real father and mother, after all—they had given me away. I was getting so mad I could hardly see straight.

"I think it's rotten," I shouted at Miss Pierce. "I think your family did a rotten thing."

"No, no," she whimpered. "Please don't yell. It never happened. Mama said it never happened. I just imagined it."

"I hate you," I yelled. "You're terrible, thinking babies are nothing." I felt if I stayed in that room a minute more I might do something awful. I tripped over a wastebasket and I felt so crazy I kicked it and ran through the door. I guess I'd been making a lot of noise, because I almost ran down Mrs. Walsh.

"Barry." She grabbed my arm. "What's all the shouting about? Is Miss Pierce all right?"

"Just leave me alone." I jerked my arm away and ran down the hall and out the front door. I kept running down the street—it's amazing I wasn't arrested on suspicion of something. I stopped when I couldn't breathe anymore, and leaned against a store window and panted. When I could finally hold my head up, I started to walk slowly, trying to ignore the people who were staring at me.

I got to Golden Gate Park and went in and sat on the first bench I could find and then—I'm almost ashamed to say it—I started to cry. I couldn't seem to stop. It was crazy—it wasn't as if I had just found out I was adopted or anything. I had known all along my real parents had put me up for adoption; people just don't go in and grab babies. I guess, though, it was the first time I ever realized that somebody had said, "We can't keep this kid, let somebody else have him." I don't know why after all that time I felt hurt, but I did.

A little kid stopped to stare at me, and his mother wanted to know if she could help. Then, an old man sat down beside me and offered me some of his squirrels' peanuts. Without thinking, I took one.

"It helps to chew," he said. "I guess it keeps the blood from getting to the brain and you can't think so much."

I tried to smile, and realized it would be as easy to start laughing as it had been to start crying and maybe I better get out of there before some doctors came to take me away. It was a long walk home, which was just as well because by the time I got to my front steps I had myself under better control. I'm sure I looked a mess, though, and I hoped my folks were out playing golf. But no such luck. Mom opened the door. From the expression on her face, I was pretty sure Mrs. Walsh had phoned and told her Barry had gone berserk, shouted at Miss Pierce, kicked a wastebasket, and left the hospital like a crazy man.

"Barry?"

"Hi, Mom," I said. I tried to cover the shake in my voice with a cough. Then my father came into the hall. He was still wearing his golf clothes.

"Barry." Mom touched my arm. "What happened?"

"Nothing," I said. I tried to get by them. I wasn't sure how long I could hold myself together.

Mom turned to look at Dad, and he nodded at her, and before I knew what happened, I found myself back out on the street. Dad had his hand under my elbow, and I had to run to keep up with him. We didn't say anything until we got to the local coffee shop, the one I hung around when I was playing at being Willie, the dirty rat.

"A coffee and a Coke," my father said to the waitress. We still hadn't said anything when the waitress banged them down on the table and went away.

·12·

"You want to talk about it?" Dad finally asked.

I wanted to say no, but even I could see I wasn't going to get away with that. "I don't know," I said.

"Mrs. Walsh seemed to think there was some problem with the old lady you've been seeing. Your mother, on the other hand, thinks it could have something to do with your being adopted. But then"— he smiled faintly—"any time anything happens with you, that's the first thing she thinks of. Barry, I want to help." He reached over and touched my hand. Now, that might not sound like a big deal to you, but we're not great huggers and touchers in our family. I sucked in my breath, afraid I was going to start crying again.

"Please," my father said. "It's so damn hard to help if I don't know what's wrong. I know you like the old lady, and Mrs. Walsh seemed to feel you had gotten interested in her family. Is that what's wrong—has the family been giving you problems, or what?"

I could see I was eventually going to have to say something, but what could I say? That a guy I had admired but never met because he had been dead for years had done something I didn't like. That I felt I wasn't worth anything because even my own parents didn't want me. I knew what he would say to that: "Don't worry, son. We love you. Now shape up and stop whining." I played around with the straw that came with the Coke, all the time aware that my father was watching me.

"Would you rather talk to your mother?" he finally asked.

I shook my head.

"Look, son, you're going to have to make up your mind to talk to somebody. I mean, you can't go screaming and yelling out of a convalescent hospital, leaving some poor old lady in tears, stay away for two hours, come home looking like the wrath of God, and then say nothing's wrong."

"Is Miss Pierce all right?" I asked. All I needed was to feel guilty about hurting her. It wasn't her fault, those things she said, and she couldn't help how Willie had acted. I liked to think if I had been in Willie's shoes I would have looked for the baby, but then I didn't see my real father and mother banging on our door.

"I'm sure she's fine. If she wasn't, we would have heard," my father said.

But he kept looking at me, and finally I gave up. I tried to tell him what upset me, without making it sound as if I didn't want him as a father or that I

124

thought my real father would be any better. Even when I'm curious about my real parents, I'm not exactly comparing them to Mom and Dad. It's more a case of wondering if I get my thick hair from them, or my weird sense of humor, or my lack of height. Did they come from a loud, noisy sort of family, or was their background more like mine now, where nobody lets it all hang out? But even my curiosity made me feel disloyal.

I summed it up by saying, "I don't know why it upset me. Except maybe I felt as if I was standing right there when they decided to give me away, or maybe it was because I suddenly could see how easy it is to give someone away." I looked up a little fearfully. I expected him to say, "We'd never give you away," and I knew that wouldn't make me feel any better because it was just something you say automatically without thinking.

But he didn't say that. He just looked at me for a long time, and then he asked, "Did you ever think of us?"

Geez, don't tell me I was going to get a lecture on selfishness? I shook my head.

"About how your mother and I feel, that maybe we're not what you would have picked out for yourself? You want to know something else? Every night I say two prayers. One is to thank God your parents gave you up for adoption." When I started to interrupt, he raised his hand. "I don't care why they did it—all that's important is that we have you. My second prayer is that you're never sorry we turned out to be the ones to get you. If sometimes I'm a little hard on you, it's because I want to be the perfect parent. I'm afraid when you're an adult you'll think I botched up your life. I'm sorry, Barry."

I gotta tell you, I started to cry again. I hoped that was it, that I'd used up all the tears—I mean, I was fourteen years old and I don't care, even with all the new jazz about guys not being afraid to show their feelings, it's embarrassing to sit in public and keep crying. It's better, though, if you have to cry, to cry with a man. Dad just sat there quietly waiting for me to stop before he handed me about three dozen paper napkins to mop myself up with. Mom would have been all over the place, creating a scene and making sure everybody in the place noticed. After I pulled myself together again, we got up and walked out, very cool-like.

We didn't say a word on the way home. I was glad Dad didn't want to keep rehashing the same thing over and over again so that after a while the whole conversation begins to sound like a very bad movie. You know, the kind that has a big scene at the end and in the last five minutes all the problems of the world are solved and everybody goes off happily into the sunset. This was very comfortable. Dad had said his piece and that was that.

Mom was banging pots and pans around in the kitchen when we came in. "Is everything all right?" She tried to make her voice sound nonchalant, but she was looking at Dad as if she expected him to tell her I was terminal.

"Everything's fine," Dad said, and thank God he didn't throw his arm around my shoulder to prove it—things were too theatrical as it was.

"Barry," Mom started, and then she looked at Dad as if expecting him to stop her. She started again. "I don't know what the problem is—" She slowed down and waited a second to see if either one of us said anything. When we didn't, she continued, "If it has something to do with us adopting you, I just want to say one thing." She looked at Dad again. "If you really want to find out who your real parents are, we understand. We wouldn't feel that you love us any less because you wanted to know where you came from." She sighed and stopped knotting the dish towel and looked at me.

I said that was awfully nice of them and maybe one day I might take them up on it, but right now I didn't think I could handle any more people. All I needed was two sets of parents to finish me off completely. If you can believe it, we then sat down to dinner as if nothing had happened. I think, though, all these raw emotions upset us, because what we talked about at dinner was who we would invite for Thanksgiving.

Mrs. Walsh called me the next day. I was going to phone her and apologize for my behavior, but I hadn't gotten around to it. I was relieved she sounded friendly, as if she wasn't planning on bawling me out.

"How is Miss Pierce?" I asked.

"Well," said Mrs. Walsh, "you seem to have shaken her up a bit." When I started to say something, she interrupted. "Don't worry, Barry. She's fine. If anything, she's not quite as confused today as she usually is. I wouldn't get my hopes up, though. She's been like this before, and eventually she slips back into the past. Anyway, I thought you might like to visit her this afternoon, reassure yourself she's all right."

I knew Mrs. Walsh probably meant well, and although I wasn't really ready to go back to Cherry Garden right then, I agreed. So, after 12:15 Mass, I went over. Before I started down the familiar hall to room 105, I looked around. I guess I had gotten used to the place because it didn't look as terrible as it had the first time I saw it. The main room was really just a large, old, untidy family room, and the old people weren't just old clothes and wheelchairs. They were all different and some of them were nice and fun to be with.

When I got to the door of Miss Pierce's room, I decided to pretend that the last visit hadn't happened. Actually, I wanted to pretend that none of the last two months had happened. Here I was, Barry Wilson, and I was going to visit an old lady as part of a class project.

She looked up when I walked in. "Who are you? Do I know you?" She was still huddled under her blankets, and her hair still stood up in crazy wisps all over her head.

"No," I said. "But I came to visit you."

When she kept looking at me, I continued, "You see, the school I go to has us visit here."

To my surprise, she simply nodded.

"From a school? What's the name of it?"

"Bishop Alemany," I replied.

"Oh." She appeared puzzled. "That sounds religious, almost like a church."

"Yes," I agreed. "It's a Catholic high school."

"With nuns?"

"Well, only a few now. Mostly we have regular teachers."

"High school, you say? You don't look old enough to be in high school."

"I'm fourteen," I said. "But I'm short for my age."

"My brother Willie always worried about being too short, but he was much taller than you. He was a very nice-looking boy."

"But he didn't have much character," I muttered under my breath.

For a few minutes, neither one of us said anything. I was racking my brain, trying to think of something else to talk about when Miss Pierce said, "I never had a visitor all my own before. Just family. Is there anything I should do? Should I give you something to eat?" She looked around as if she expected food magically to appear.

"No, we can just talk if you like."

"I'm not good at talking to people. What do you want to talk about? Willie always knew how to talk to people, but Mama said I was silly and shy."

A few days ago, I would have jumped at the chance to talk about Willie, but now I didn't care if I ever heard his name again. "Would you like to go for a walk?" I asked.

"That would be nice. My brother, Willie, when we were young, often would take me out."

I propped open the door with my foot and maneuvered her wheelchair out into the hall. It seemed to me that no matter how confused she was, it couldn't hurt to have her see something besides the four walls of her room. Taking her out and trying to get her into the present made me feel a little less guilty about yelling and screaming at her. Mrs. Walsh should be pleased I was helping to orientate her. I pushed her chair down to the activity room, but it was full of people and Miss Pierce didn't like that. The dining room was empty, so I took her in there.

"This is nice," she said. "I like it better where it's quiet. When I was little, we had a big house that had a garden, and I used to play out there by myself." She sighed. "It was a lovely house just perfect for children. Of course, I didn't get married, and poor Willie died so young, so there weren't any children to play there anymore." She frowned a little, as if something she was saying didn't quite fit.

I guess, in a way, it made sense to her, and in time she had come to believe there had never been a baby at all. Maybe she had forgotten about Teresa, too. It was spooky. If I hadn't seen the marriage license and the certificate of baptism, I would never have questioned her story.

We sat quietly for a few minutes, and then she turned to me. "You look familiar somehow. Have you ever visited me here before? I have trouble

130

remembering things—have I forgotten you?"

"No," I said. It was better that way. Who wants to be told they keep forgetting things?

"That's good," she said. "Because you seem like a very nice boy, and I wouldn't want to hurt your feelings."

We talked for a few more minutes, until Mrs. Walsh came along looking for Miss Pierce because it was time for her medicine.

When I said goodbye, she smiled and grabbed my hand. "You'll come visit me again, won't you? I get so lonely." Then she thanked me for such a pleasant afternoon.

. . .

It would have been nice if she hadn't called me Willie for the rest of the semester, but it didn't happen that way. There were good days when she was Miss Pierce and she told me stories about the San Francisco she remembered; there were bad days when she wanted me to be Willie and I wouldn't be.

Jim gave another puppet show at Thanksgiving, and he tried to make it more adult. Ms. Jackson helped him with the script, and everybody gave him a nice round of applause. The band came and they started out being terrible, but then Mr. Hollis suggested they play some melodies that people could sing to and everybody enjoyed that. I gave an oral report on how people can remember lyrics to old songs but forget what day it is. Rory got the girls who were working at the day-care center to bring their kids over. They had made paper turkeys to give the residents, and, even better, they climbed up on people's laps and asked for glasses of water and rides in wheelchairs. All of the old people had candy to give the children, and Rory gave a report on how much it meant to the elderly to still be able to give.

Mom knitted Miss Pierce a new blanket for Christmas, but she gave it to me to bring to her. We had a big Christmas party at the hospital, and then we, the kids, went on Christmas vacation. When school started up again after the first of the year, there were only a few weeks left of the class. I had a terrible time writing my report, and when I was finished, it didn't really say anything important, just a bunch of garbage about loneliness and how the project gave us a better feeling about old people.

Even though the class is over now, Rory and I plan to keep visiting. Of course, Rory went over to Cherry Garden even before the project, so I'm sure everyone expected her to go on doing that, but I was surprised to find I wanted to continue seeing Miss Pierce. She seems to look forward to my visits, even if some days she doesn't know me. I never ask about Willie, and if she mentions him or calls me Willie, I just change the subject. I hope some nice people adopted the baby and he had a good life, but there's nothing I can do about it. You know, though, sometimes when I see Miss Pierce just sitting there in her wheelchair,

I remember those pictures of her and Willie and think about how much she loved him, and I'm sorry things didn't turn out better. But then nobody's perfect, not even Willie.